MW01241652

But I Have Known You

To Doug,

Never enough books!

Judith Joyce Poe

Judith Joyce Poe

11/05

PublishAmerica

Baltimore

© 2002 by Judith Ann Poe.
All rights reserved. No part of this book may be reproduced, stored in a retrieval system or transmitted in any form or by any means without the prior written permission of the publishers, except by a reviewer who may quote brief passages in a review to be printed in a newspaper, magazine or journal.

First printing

This book is a work of fiction. Names, characters, places, and incidents are the product of the author's imagination and are used fictitiously. Any resemblance to actual events, locales, or persons, living or dead is coincidental.

ISBN: 1-59286-447-3
PUBLISHED BY PUBLISHAMERICA, LLLP
www.publishamerica.com
Baltimore

Printed in the United States of America

This book is dedicated to my husband, Charles, who has been my mentor and helpmate throughout the writing of it, and, indeed, the whole of our life together.

ACKNOWLEDGMENTS

It is with a wealth of thanks that I recognize the following people who have helped with the support and encouragement all along the path in the creation of *But I Have Known You.*

For all the reference items that I have requested and the timely manner in which I was served, I thank Diana Tucker. She has been a miracle worker.

To all those people at PublishAmerica who have made a dream come true, I thank you.

To the friends who have critiqued the book, Millie Crisco, Joan Arft, Jane Wall, Caroline Hoffman, Regina Poe, Debra Wade, Pamela Schroeder, Margie Marden, Jane Kummer, John and Ann Higginbotham, Dorothy Kuhlmann, and Patty Sims, I thank you for your encouragement and comments.

To my sister writers, Bobbie Smith and Julie Beard, who have read *But I Have Known You* in part or in whole, I thank you for your insights.

PROLOGUE

December 30, 1847

She heard the voices of Daniel and the doctor growing fainter and quieter as they descended the stairs toward the front hall. It was warm here in her room with Jonathan cuddled in her arms, she hated to let him go. His dark hair curled so like his father's and his short black eyelashes promised to become the luxurious ones of the future. But her arms were growing tired, and there was one last thing she had to do before she slept. Motioning to the nurse who sat nearby on a chair, she lifted the child to her without a word, watching as she gently lay him in the cradle by her bed.

Then, beckoning for the nurse to bend down, she whispered in her ear, "Please bring me paper, pen, and ink, I must lay something to paper before I sleep."

"But, miss, you need your rest now after your ordeal."

"And, I will, to be sure, but first the things I need. Also bring a sharp knife and some mucilage, you'll find them in the top drawer of my secretary across the room by the window."

The nurse hurried to gather the materials and place them on the bed along with a small bed desk for the invalid.

Catherine looked at the paper as if gathering her thoughts and then began to write.

December 30, 1847

Dear Edgar,

> *I know that you are unaware of the birth of your son, and so, I enclose the birth certificate that the doctor has filled out for me, which I know you will safeguard. Please do not be angry with me for taking your name. I know we*

7

would be married if you had been aware of the existence of Jonathan. I wanted you to come to me of your own accord because you loved me and not because of a fatherly duty to your son or me. And so I did not write before now. Please care for him if anything should happen to me. Remember my love for you is "timeless."

Yours forever,
Cathy

Putting the birth certificate and letter inside the cover of the book she held and repairing the inside cover she place it beneath her pillows. She felt herself slipping into sleep.

The nurse cleared the writing materials away and resumed her vigil over the mother and child.

September 15, 2001

"Meredith kept everything, didn't she?" Penny asked as she was sorting through the closets and drawers.

"What in the world do you think she was saving this old suitcase for?" Denise inquired as she tugged an old brown suitcase from the back of the closet into the middle of the room. It was dirty and scarred from years of being pushed from one place to another. Upon opening the lid, there, in confusion and disarray, lay hundreds of old photos, some from the late nineteenth century. And under all the pictures of first communions and World War I uniformed men, lay a book. It looked like it had seen better days as well. The corners were dog-eared and worn, the cover, though it was leather, was greasy and crusted with dirt. It had been left, as had the pictures, in the suitcase unremembered by the family at large. Only Meredith had known who most of the people in the photos were or who might have written the book. And now that Meredith Montgomery Warren was dead, there was no one left to ask.

"Do you think that there is any reason to keep all this stuff? I don't know anything about them, do you?" Denise asked.

"No, and I don't think it would do any good to ask Bruce or Ruth, they were hardly home enough to look at the recent stuff, much less know anything about any of this," Penny said.

"Okay, then I am going to put these on the sale table for the auction next week. Maybe someone wants an instant ancestor or something. Might as well make a buck on them instead of throwing them in the trash," Denise said pulling a box to her and placing the photos in it.

She looked at the book again; inside the front cover was an inscription to someone named Jonathan from his mother with instructions to give the book to his father when he came. She didn't know anyone named Jonathan in the family, it must be something her stepmother had seen at a sale and decided she had to have. Her stepmother had always loved poetry, and leafing through a few pages, she saw that it was indeed a book of poetry.

She separated the book into another box that had old books from the library that they had decided to get rid of. Her stepmother had kept everything and now it was up to them to get rid of it. She brushed the hair from her forehead and sighed. Why hadn't Meredith gotten rid of these things before now? Why hang on to all of this? She guessed she might have, if she hadn't died so suddenly. Now it was she and Penny's job to do it.

Well, best be finishing up with the job, as the auction was scheduled for next weekend and they still had the basement and attic to go through. What a job, they had been at it now for four days and there was another four to go. It had been six months since Meredith had passed; now the time was rushing up on them, the house had been sold, and they needed to vacate before the new owners came to take possession.

CHAPTER ONE

October 1957

Autumn and unseasonably warm, the heat rose in waves from the rooftops of the houses, shimmering and quiet. The weather felt unsettled as though a storm might be brewing somewhere far off and was approaching the town slowly and with purpose. On the small street, in a white frame house, sat a girl in the bloom of her youth. She had lived in this house on this street with her two brothers, mother, and stepfather for four years, probably the longest time in one place since her mother had remarried. She had studied in this room at this desk all that time. And this was the first time that she was in a quandary. It was the first test of her junior year geometry class.

Marissa brushed her fine flyaway hair from her eyes and took up her book again, trying to make sense out of the words in the heat. No matter how long she looked at it or how hard she tried, she just couldn't make sense of the problems she was trying to master. Why was it so hard for her to fathom? When the line went from point A to point B to point D, why couldn't she find point C? She would have to get help with it, she knew that, but who to ask without feeling stupid. Her mother hadn't completed the 10th grade, she wouldn't be able to help her and her stepfather would only make her uncomfortable if she asked him. He was forever trying to touch her and get closer to her. She didn't like it. No, she didn't like it at all. Would her mother believe her if she told her about his advances, probably not. And if she did, what could she do about it? Best just keep as much distance between her stepfather and herself as she could.

She would ask one of her friends for help. So she called up her friend, Elaine, and they made a date to study that weekend and then go to a movie together. It would help to get out of the house and away from Sam. Marissa was lonely now that her steady boyfriend had gone away to college and she was feeling restless and craving some activity. A study time and a movie with friends seemed just the answer to both her problems.

It was later that same evening and Elaine was driving to the drive-in theater when she asked, "Marissa, when are you going to see Jim again?"

"I don't know," said Marissa, "I had hoped he would call this weekend but I haven't heard a word and then I guessed he had too much studying to do, like I did."

"I think you are so lucky to be going with him."

"I suppose so, but it sure isn't the same as last year when we saw each other every day at school."

They parked the car and began to watch the movie. It was one of the new thriller movies where the hero had cars racing down hills and being blown up while he miraculously survived. The two girls were watching intently and did not notice that the empty spot next to them had been filled or that the car that had pulled in beside them had its window rolled down. It was a sleek looking sedan that looked vaguely familiar when they looked over at it as though they had seen it at the market or in the school parking lot. The people inside looked familiar too, and Marissa remembered where she had seen the driver before. He was in her study hall at school. He was a senior there while she was just a lowly junior.

She remembered feeling his eyes on her that week in study hall and wondered who he was. Her friends had said that his name was Stephen McGuire and that he was one of the coolest guys around and drove this really cool car.

He was attractive, that was obvious. He was very dark as though he had creole ancestry, with dark brown curly hair and smoldering black eyes, and a smile that was slow and lazy and lit up his face when he gifted you with it. He always had a bunch of guys hanging around him and they obviously enjoyed each other's company. He was with one of them now.

The rumor had it that he had just broken up with one of the most attractive girls in his class. Marissa wondered whether it was true about the girl and whether it had been her idea or his to break up.

Marissa left the car and went to the snack bar for refreshments and when she returned she saw Stephen McGuire motioning for her to come over and talk.

"Hi, there, Marissa."

"Hello."

"Do you know my friend here, Tim Anderson?" Stephen asked.

"No, I don't think I do. Hello Tim."

"Hi," Tim answered.

11

Stephen looked at Marissa for a long steady moment and then said, "Tim would like to talk with Elaine for a while, would you sit here with me while they visit?"

Marissa couldn't see the harm in just sitting there with him. "Okay, I suppose it is all right."

Stephen opened the door and Marissa slid in the front seat beside him. There was a long empty silence and then Stephen turned to her and said, "Marissa, you know I have wanted to speak to you at school for a long time."

"Why didn't you?"

"Well, because everyone said you were Jim's girl and I don't cut in on someone else's girl." Marissa thought about the statement and decided that she wanted to pursue the thought. There was something about him that made her want to know him better.

"And if I weren't Jim's girl, what then?"

"I don't know," replied Stephen, "that would be up to you."

Marissa felt a warmth stealing over her, something very different than she had ever felt before, like quicksilver flooding through her veins, not even in her dreams about Jim had she felt like this.

Suddenly she knew that this boy was going to mean more to her than Jim or anyone would. She sat there beside him, this boy who was more than a boy, who was perhaps the first real man she had ever known. She wanted to be held by him, kissed by him, and have him tell her that he loved her more than anyone or anything else. But she was powerless to say any of these things. How could she feel this way about someone she barely knew? Where had this lightning flash come from? She knew that she would not willingly separate from him that evening.

They finished watching the movie and found by the end of the time that they were holding each other's hands ever so gently but firmly. He asked, "May I drive you home?"

Marissa looked into his eyes spellbound and whispered, "Yes."

He leaned out the window calling to Elaine, "Elaine, Marissa is going home with me, can you give Tim a ride?"

Elaine looked at her incredulously. "Are you sure you know what you are doing?"

"Yes, I am sure," Marissa smiled, "never more sure of anything in my life."

It was on the drive home though that she began to wonder if she really did know what she was doing. She was, after all, lavaliered to Jim, and even though Elaine was her friend, she was sure that Jim would know as soon as Elaine could get home and call her boyfriend Larry who was also at the college.

All Marissa knew was that she was going to have to call Jim in the morning and tell him that she couldn't go steady with him any longer. That would be a hard call to make. But she was sure now that she wanted to be free to see Stephen again.

Sure enough in the morning when she called Jim she could tell by the sound of his voice that someone had beat her to the call.

"Hello, Jim."

"Hello, Marissa."

"Jim, I have something to tell you, and I know you are not going to understand because I really don't understand myself, but all I know is that I can't go steady with you any longer."

"I knew you were going to call, but I really didn't want to believe it, Marissa. I thought we were in love, you said you loved me."

"I know I did and I am truly sorry that I misled you. I thought I did love you but now I know that I wasn't truly in love with you. I only thought I was. I hope you can forgive me someday. I just don't want to go steady or be lavaliered anymore, and it isn't fair to you, either. You might meet someone really nice." Marissa whispered, "I really hope you do."

"You know you can always count on me, Marissa, and if things don't work out or you find that you do feel something for me, please call me. Please give me another chance."

"Jim, I appreciate that, you are wonderful and far better than I deserve. I hope we can continue to be friends, but I don't want you to wait for me in the hopes that something might work out. You need to find someone you can love who loves you as much as you love them," she implored again.

"All right," Jim replied, "if that's how you feel, I understand, but it doesn't make it any easier. Thanks for calling anyway, even though your friends beat you to it."

"Jim, please don't hate me."

"Goodbye, Marissa."

"Goodbye, Jim."

It was several weeks later in the house on Regent Street, when the phone rang. Marissa, who was baby-sitting her little brother, Richard, picked up the receiver.

"Hello."

The voice on the other end of the line replied, "Marissa, this is Stephen. Are you busy, can you talk?"

"Yes. How are you?"

"Maybe I should ask you how you are instead?" Stephen says.

"I'm fine, sitting here baby-sitting Richard."

"Who is Richard and would you like company?"

"Richard is my baby brother and I would love company, but I think my mom and stepfather would frown on your being here when they got home."

"Well, when can I see you again or do you want to see me?" Stephen asked. "I heard from the grapevine at school that you have broken up with Jim. I'd hoped it was because you wanted to see me again."

"Yes, I'd like to see you again…. There's a basketball game this Friday after school, perhaps we could go for a soda afterwards," Marissa suggested.

"That's a date. I will expect you at school at the game. See you then."

"Okay, goodbye, Stephen."

She slowly lowered the receiver and went over and over the conversation in her mind. It was almost too good to be true that Stephen really did want to see her again. She had had a rough time at school the past weeks over the way in which she had broken up with Jim and she was feeling blue. The phone call from Stephen was just what she had needed. She knew that the feelings that she had experienced when she was with him were real and the intensity of her emotions was a little frightening. She hoped that Stephen really felt the same about her. Only time would tell and she had plenty of that. Would she be the right one for him? She prayed that he would tell her it was so.

Friday night, the night of the basketball game, came and even though Marissa had seen Stephen in the halls at school during that week, he had not spoken to her or given her any indication that he noticed her at all. Perhaps he wouldn't even remember their date, but he was here because she had seen him come into the auditorium with his friends and climb up to the grandstands to watch the game. Wasn't he going to sit beside her? Wouldn't he even talk with her? Why was he acting this way? Didn't he know that she was miserable when she felt he didn't care? The game played on and even though she cheered at the appropriate times, her heart wasn't in it. She didn't understand what she had done to deserve this treatment, but her Irish temper was beginning to bubble, when, as she was starting to leave the auditorium, she felt a hand take her arm and there he was guiding her to the door.

"Hey, were you going to leave without me." Stephen grinned at her mischievously.

"No, but I thought perhaps you had changed your mind," Marissa said pensively, her feelings showing on the sleeve of her sweater.

"Oh, come on, let's go somewhere quiet and talk over a soda or a burger or something."

"Okay, let's go." Marissa was overjoyed. He hadn't forgotten, he did want to be with her, but why the cold shoulder all evening? She didn't understand and was too afraid of angering him to ask. Perhaps it was just his way. But she was hurt and worried. Maybe she had made a mistake, perhaps he didn't feel have the same feelings as she did. Perhaps it was all a game for him. She knew some men were like that though she hadn't really had any experience with them.

They went outside and climbed in Stephen's car. It was a really nice car lowered almost to the ground with an engine that purred like a kitten under the hood. Sitting in the seat next to him, all her cares dropped away. It was almost magical, like being inside a bubble and knowing others were there but not being touched by them. She wished it could continue forever. They went to the soda shop and bought their drinks and sat for hours talking about nothing and everything, growing closer. Later driving home, he slipped his arm around her shoulder while he drove and curled her against him. Marissa could have driven forever that night and every night after that if possible. Too soon they came to her home and stopped the car at the curb. Marissa knew that she should jump right out but the look in his eyes fanned the desire growing inside her.

"Marissa, will you kiss me goodnight?" Stephen asked in a low voice.

"Yes," she whispered.

She melted into his arms. It was safe and warm and thrilling to be held by Stephen. She loved kissing him and feeling his arms tighten around her, crushing her to him. If only this could go on forever. As he began to slowly caress her arms and cupped her face to his, Marissa forced herself away from Stephen. She was shaken to her core, she could tell that Stephen wanted more. But she knew that "good" girls didn't go all the way and she was determined to save herself for the man she would marry. She hoped that someday that would be Stephen. She was surprised at her feelings for they had literally overwhelmed her from the moment she had been with him at the drive-in theater and now after this time together, she was convinced of how she felt. As long as she wasn't sure of his feelings for her, though, she hesitated telling him all these things. She would wait and see if he came calling again. They were much too young to make a commitment now. And so she struggled to compose herself and said, "I think that we better say goodnight now."

He looked at her closely to see if she was serious. "Are you sure you want to go in?"

"I am sure I had better go." She grinned. "Before I get myself in over my head."

He walked her to the door, and after a final goodnight kiss, saw her go inside.

Then turning, he strolled down the walk of her house and got into his car and drove away.

Marissa tiptoed down the hall trying not to wake her mother. But she was not successful and her mother came into her room to see how the wonderful date had gone. Somehow this was something that she was not ready to share with Veronica; she wanted to keep this private for a while and so begged sleepiness and readied herself for bed. As she lay her head down, she drifted back to the safe place that she had felt snuggled next to Stephen on the front seat of his car. She wrapped herself in the memory and closed her eyes in sleep.

Stephen drove home slowly, savoring the moments before when he had held Marissa in his arms. Could he believe in her? She was mass of confusion, first she kissed him like he had never been kissed before, then she pushed him away when he tried to caress her. What was going on in that head of hers? Was this some kind of game she was playing? He didn't know her well enough yet to know what thoughts were going through her head. But one thing he did know, she could unlock passion from within him that he hadn't known was there. Man, what a woman, he could hardly keep his hands off of her, and perhaps he had frightened her a little. He hadn't meant to press so hard but his whole being trembled still at the feel of her skin and the heat of her lips. She was so beautiful and vulnerable, even though she tried to put on this strong uncaring act, he could almost see the scars left by some childhood hurts. He didn't know yet what they were, but he would find out and heal them if he could. He thought he loved her, but he wouldn't let her know that yet. That would give away too much power and she had the power to hurt him, too, if he let her. He'd wait and see. The lights of the oncoming traffic jerked him out of his reverie and he saw his turn coming up. Slowing the car to take the left, he pulled into the driveway of his parents' home and shut it off, still sitting in his car musing over the evening. Yes, he'd wait and see.

CHAPTER TWO

July 26, 1940

Screaming, kicking, bright red and squirming, she was pulled from her mother's womb by cold metal forceps and brought into the light of the world. She was two weeks late, in addition to being breech birth (which meant that if she ever wanted to find water, all she would need to do would be to find a water witches' wand, another name for a forked stick, and point it to the ground). Or so the old wive's tales say. Her mother lay as still as death as the doctors hurried to repair the damage they had done to her. The nurses swathed the child in clean blankets and hurried her off to the nursery. She wanted her mother, not those busy white-dressed women who hustled and bustled in and out of the nursery with bottles, diapers and clean blankets. No one had time for her. No one would hold her and rock her and comfort her. She wanted her mother.

July 26, 1825

Where was her mother? She cried and cried on the way to this place and still her mother did not come? She was hungry and tired and she wanted her mother. Why did she have to get in the carriage and ride all this way? Why couldn't she see her mother anywhere, she was there when she was born, but where had they taken her and what happened to her mother? She wanted her mother!

August 9, 1940

They named her "Marissa Suellen Joeleen." Her mother, Veronica, thought it was a fancy sounding name and that she would grow into it. Maybe she did and maybe she didn't but at that time it didn't matter. All that mattered was her mom and her touch.

She, like everyone, remembered only that at an early age they are hot or cold, wet or dry, hungry or not hungry. Except, of course, for those things her mother later told her, like being the only baby to take an 8-ounce bottle at her first feeding and having very large fingers and toes. But since those things have persisted, she would have been aware of them from the first. Where was her father? Why didn't he hold her like her mother did? Didn't he like her? Perhaps she wasn't pretty enough? She loved her mother, but she longed for her father to hold her.

August 9, 1825

She is always talking to her, trying to get her to drink this stuff, it's not too bad, but it isn't her mother's milk. She would know that milk, but this is better than nothing; so she would have to drink it. The woman keeps her pretty dry, too, it wasn't too bad here, but they better give her back to her mother or they will be very sorry. She would sleep now, that stuff the woman makes her drink makes her warm and sleepy. She isn't her mother or her father, but she is nice to her. What happened to her father, where is he and why doesn't he come for her?

August 1943

She scarcely remembered her father, he was never around much. She was two when her baby brother came, so she didn't remember much of her mother's second pregnancy. However, she did remember her baby brother. The one who cried all the time and took up all of mother's energy and time. He was pretty sick when he was born, they stuck needles in his head and gave him medicines, she heard her mother tell her father, and Mother was pretty worried most of the time. She knew she didn't much like him then or she wouldn't have slammed the window down on his little fingers. My, my, what a naughty child she was turning into. Maybe that was the reason why, when Daddy finally left and Mother had to care for them, she was sent to live with her grandparents. Perhaps she was too mean to live with her brother.

But with the day of coming to Grandma and Grandpa's, life became effortless and new. They gave her the love and affection that every child needs. Days were filled with hair brushing and tooth brushing, with the awful grainy white powder called baking soda, though why they called it soda was beyond her, she had had soda and it was great stuff.

There was bathing on Saturday night in the porcelain bathtub with two or three inches of water and a crocheted washcloth which was shaped like a turtle, filled with Ivory soap, which kept swimming out of her reach. Her grandmother would heat the buckets of water on the stove and fill the tub with as much hot water as she could carry in two buckets adding a little cold from the taps. The cold porcelain would quickly chill the water before she even stepped into it and she would sit trying to wash and clean herself without her teeth chattering in her head. It was going to be a bone of contention in later years, to always have the tub as full as she could get it with as hot a water as she could stand. So hot, she would rise flushed and red as though she had been boiled as a lobster into hot water.

The house on Elm Street, where they lived, was not large by most standards, just four rooms and a cold water bath. Not even plumbing for the toilet, her grandpa had to take care of the waste from that, and there was a pantry off the kitchen with a trapdoor leading down into the cellar. There, in the winter, one could hear the roaring of the coal-fired furnace and she would stand over the heat registers with her gown ballooning in the early mornings before school. She used to peek downstairs when Grandpa went below to fire the furnace and see him shoveling in huge shovels of coal and the roaring fire in the open grate looked like what the hell that the preacher used to talk about on Sunday morning might be like. It was always dark and scary down there and it was only on Monday mornings it seemed like a good place when she would stand to help Grandma do the wash.

There were interesting things in that house, too, most of which she was not supposed to see or touch. Like the beautiful crocheted doilies that adorned the backs of all the chairs and table tops, created by the nimble fingers of her grandma. She would watch her sit in the evenings by the radio with her crippled fingers flying at the thread and hook. It seemed that magic made the loops and circles of thread become spider webs of beauty for the tables and chair backs.

September 1825

She watched as the woman's fingers pulled the thread back and forth and back and forth through the cloth. It was mesmerizing to watch her. Mathilda continued for quite a time and then looked at Catherine with a smile on her face.

"You don't know what I am doing, do you, lovey?" she said. "Why I am repairing your clothes so you don't go naked, sweets. Now you lie there in your cradle by the fire and take a little sleep."

It was warm in the cradle in front of the fire, and as she sewed she pushed the stave of the cradle and it began to rock. Catherine, lulled by the warmth of the fire and gentle rocking motion, slowly drifted back to sleep.

The man had been adamant about her ability to care for the child. She was to tell her nothing about her parents or background until she was grown or Mathilda was near to death herself. There would be no rewards for either of them if the girl were to try to establish a relationship with the mother. He was seeing to her education and welfare (against his better judgement) in placing her with Matilda but if she attempted to locate her parents or him, he would cut them both off without a dime.

Matilda couldn't understand why he was so uncaring and cruel, but she had longed for a child of her own and since she'd never married, had given up hope of ever having one. No, he could be sure that Catherine would be loved and cared for, not because of any reward either. She could already tell the child would be a beauty. She would protect her with her life.

July 1945

In Grandpa's room next to the window that looked out on the porch, there was the small smoke stand. It was filled with little bags of funny smelling stuff and matchboxes and papers and things. She was never supposed to touch those things and, of course, she never did, until much, much later. She would sit on the large front porch that looked onto the street, in a porch swing where she would laze in the hot summer. Not much went on living on her street that she didn't know about, but occasionally a child would go by or an infrequent car and once a week the iceman would come with his delivery of ice, followed usually right after by the milkman with his milk and butter.

The iceman had his horse and cart and carried large chunks of ice for the iceboxes of the houses. She would gaze at the horse and wish that she were big enough to walk outside the fence and pet the animal. It would stand quietly in the traces and wait for the return of the driver to pull forward to another house, and so it went, until they turned the corner, and she could glimpse them no more.

By and large, it was a happy time. There weren't too many children to play with, only a girl about Marissa's age across the street who had lost her mother and lived with her father. She could never ever go to her house, though; the girl could only come to hers. Marissa must never leave the yard with anyone except her grandma or grandpa. It seems funny to her now, she couldn't go next door or across the street to play, but her grandparents would let her be taken many miles away by someone (his name was Sam) who was almost a stranger to her. She had seen him with her mother. Marissa was allowed to spend the whole day at his mother's house. Why would they do that, do you think? Was it because he was spending a lot of time with her mother now? Perhaps they thought she should get to know the people she might become related to, or did they just trust him to take care of her? Whatever the reason, it was a short visit and she was returned home to her grandma safe and sound after all.

Close around the corner was a graveyard, which had a lot of open space and she remembered going there to fly a kite with her grandpa. It was a box kite that he had made for her, spending many hours cutting the wood and nailing and gluing it together. Then covering it with paper (one of the old-fashioned kind) and she needed so much tail that it would hardly stay aloft. She remembered flying it with Grandpa with the wind in her straight brown hair and a smile on her face. These times with her grandpa were special to her. Often in the evenings Grandpa would come in with the newspaper and sit on his bed with her beside him to hear him read the funnies. Yes, these were the special times, in later years she would still be able to hear his voice and her own in laughter.

July 1829

That man is here again, she doesn't like him. He stares at her with the dark look on his face and she can tell he doesn't like her. She usually hid behind Mathilda's skirts but sometimes she drags her out to show her off to him. She would rather be outside in the sunshine walking in the grass than in here with him staring at her. Thank goodness he doesn't stay long, just gives Mathilda a purse and her another stare and then off he goes again. She hoped he never came back.

September 1948

She saw her mother now and then, but not every day or even every other day. She worked nights teaching dancing at the Arthur Murray Dance Studio and sleeping days and taking care of her brother. Her brother spent more time with strangers than she did and perhaps that is why he suffered later on in life with bouts of extreme depression and fatigue; she didn't think he ever felt he belonged anywhere. He was a teasing friendly child, a needy child who craved attention. All boy and full of fun, he was stocky with beautiful blond hair that glistened in the sunlight like spun gold. He suffered early on from rickets, which left him knock-kneed and he needed to be exposed to the sun at all opportunities. So he would come to romp and play at Grandma's in the summer sunshine and he and Marissa would fight and play. Every time they were together they would be up to some kind of mischief. But somehow they came to know that they could always depend on each other if the chips were down. If they couldn't be together all the time, then they would make up for it later.

The days bubbled along one pretty much like the other, until one day her mother came to see her. She looked so beautiful and distant. She told her that she was going to be gone for a long time. Marissa was to stay with Grandma and Grandpa. Be a good girl until she returned. She was not to worry, Veronica would be back for her. She didn't understand then what her mother meant by being gone, because she was gone most the time anyway but Marissa agreed to be good. What else could she be? Her grandma and grandpa made sure that she was well cared for and fed, why would she act out? Her grandma rubbed her back at night until she fell asleep listening to the paperboys hawking their papers. While she slept beside her in the quiet night, what ever would she fear?

June 1831

"Mamma, are you my real grandma?" Catherine asked as Mathilda sat combing out her curly black hair.

"No, my sweet, but I love you like you were my own grandchild," Mathilda answered.

Catherine sat and thought about that for a while and then turning her gray blue eyes on to her mamma, she said, "What happened to my real grandparents? And who is my real mother and father?" the child questioned waiting for the answer, but fearing it as well.

"I don't know them," Mathilda lied, because, of course, she did but had vowed silence for her's and the child's protection.

"But how did I come to live with you?" Catherine persisted.

"Does is really matter all that much how you came to be here, can't you just accept that you are and be happy, child?" the woman replied.

"I guess it doesn't really matter, if they had loved me they wouldn't have given me up, would they?" Her eyes misted and it broke Mathilda's heart to bring pain to the child.

"Just be happy, Catherine, aren't you warm, and clothed, and loved, here with me?"

"Oh yes, Mamma, I wouldn't be anywhere else, but sometimes I wonder that's all." Catherine tried to mend the hurt that she saw in Mathilda's eyes. But still she longed for a father's arms to hold her and let her know that she was loved. Would she ever have that? Perhaps someday, her father would come on a white horse and tell her that he had been searching for her all his life, that an evil king had kidnapped her and now that he had found her they would live happily ever after.

Mathilda watched the thoughts play across the child's face and tried to keep her happy. But, yes, all children long for the security of a family, mother and father, to keep them safeguarded. She hoped someday Catherine would have that in her own life.

September 1948

Mother had been gone a long time, and whenever she had asked her grandma when she was coming back to see her, she would only say that

Mother had gone to California and would be home sometime and not to worry, wasn't she taking care of her okay? And, of course, she was, so she would shrug her shoulders and nod her head in agreement. The picture in her mind of her mother was dimming and she needed to see her. There were no photo books to look at and so she waited. She wouldn't have to wait too much longer.

"Marissa," Grandma called, "come here a moment, dear."

She was outside doing the thing she loved most, swinging on her swing under the trees in the side yard. The sun was shining down through the leaves and creating dapple patterns of shade on the ground and her. At one point in apex of her swing, it would sparkle in her eyes, causing her to blink the quick tears back while the wind of swinging helped to dry them on her cheeks. School had just started a couple of weeks before so she could not get enough of playing outside when she could. She had homework to do as second grade had just begun, but the swing had beckoned to her when she came up the street from school and she just wanted to swing the day away. She began to drag her feet on the ground each time she came back and forth to slow herself down and pretty soon she jumped off the swing and ran to the back door to see why she had been called.

When she entered the house, she knew at once that something was different. Her mother was sitting at the kitchen table and she had a very serious look on her face. She ran to her to get a hug and she held her tight and kissed her. Marissa couldn't wait to tell her mother that she had been chosen for the Indian Princess in the school play. Perhaps she could come and watch. Before she could get the words out of her mouth, her mother blurted, "Marissa, honey, I have gotten married again." She was shocked, of course; she knew her mother had a boyfriend, his name was Sam, but she didn't think that it was that serious. Although at seven years old, what did she know? She was happy for her because she seemed to be happy about it but what did that have to do with her? she wondered.

She was soon to find out. Her grandma was wiping at her eyes and looking at her strangely. What was going on? Then grandma sat down and took her hand and looked closely at her.

"Marissa," she said, "your mother wants you to come and live with her now, with her and her new husband and Ryan. It is up to you, dear, you can say where you want to live."

What was going to happen to her, should she stay with her grandma and grandpa or go to live with her brother and mother and new stepfather? She wouldn't be in the school play if she left to go with them, she wouldn't see her grandma and grandpa much either, but somehow the look on her mother's face decided for her. She would have to go with her, she needed her to go with her, she could tell that it was so. She would have to leave her grandma's arms. She could see the tears welling into Grandma's eyes as she waited for her to speak. How could she leave her, it was too much for a small child to have to decide. She struggled to understand her feelings; somehow she knew her mother and her brother needed her. That much she did know, though how she knew she had no idea. Perhaps it was a premonition for the future but whatever it was she would have to go.

"I will come with you, Mama," she said very slowly and soberly with just the slightest tremble to her lips. Her grandma held her close as Marissa tried to let her know how much she would miss her, too.

September 1835

"Why do I have to leave you, mamma?" she cried. "I don't want to go to an old school far away, why can't I stay here with you?" She sat twisting her hair and worrying her skirt. Her mamma (which she had learned to call her and it seemed to make Mathilda happy) was brushing her hair and helping her pack her clothes.

"It will just be during the school year, Cathy, and you will be home again for summer, do not fret so, I will be here waiting for you when you return with the sweet tarts that you love and your room all ready. Now don't fuss so, I have taught you all I can but you must learn more and become educated. I love you sweetling, but you must go, and I must let you go, off to school. Now don't embarrass me by acting out and mind your teachers when they instruct and prepare you for your life ahead."

"Yes, Mamma," she sniffed, "but I will miss you so!"

"Perhaps right at first you might, but then your head will be so full of learning and there are other girls there for you to study with, you will soon get used to being without your mamma."

"I will never get used to being without you, Mamma. I love you!"

April 1949

"Come on, Marissa," Ryan yelled, "there are some great things down here."

Ryan was on the huge pile of broken glass and trash covering the backside of the hill behind the house where her stepfather had moved them. She was in a new school and learning the ins and outs of being in a new family. Her brother was getting into mischief as usual, and as usual she was right behind him. There was creek at the bottom of the hill and a grassy area around it. They would push blocks of wood for boats in the water and poke through the trash looking for colored glass and money and nails and screws, anything that could become treasure for their hunts.

"Ryan," Marissa replied, "you better not tear your pants again or you will get us both in trouble. You know how Sam is about the money it costs to clothe us."

"I won't tear my pants. I found a nickel under this bottle and there are more over there, just look for yourself."

"Just be careful, if you fall you might cut yourself."

"You are the one who might fall, look behind you."

"Where? Oh, I can't keep my balance. Help Ryan, I'm falling!" Marissa tumbled backwards into the heap of trash that Ryan had indicated. She felt a sharp pain in her back and then nothing, she could not move and she shouted, "Ryan, call Mom. I can't get up. Hurry, I think I'm hurt," Marissa groaned.

Ryan ran screaming into the house to get Mom. It seemed like forever that Marissa lay there, but finally over the top of the hill a head appeared and Marissa's mother called to her.

"Marissa, can you move your legs?"

"Yes, Mom, but I don't think I can get up."

The ambulance arrived with the paramedics carrying a long board to help load her into the back. It was dark in the ambulance and the people there kept telling her to lie still and they would be at the hospital soon. Too soon came the doctor's poking and prodding and finally they put her under the x-ray machine. But no serious injury could be found and it was decided that a day or two in bed would solve the problem. And it did, for on the morning of the second day, she found she could stand and walk and nothing untoward seemed to be happening. Perhaps some discomfort on sitting and rising, but that too faded with time. Of course, Ryan was blamed for them being on the trash heap even though she was the older of them and should have prevented them both from being there.

Schools came and schools went as the family moved, first from one location after another, always it seemed further and further away from her grandparents. Each move brought new vistas and new children to meet and sometimes new relatives.

She had never lived in a place like this before. The last place they had lived in had had a back yard and a front yard and sat on its yards like a chair on a throne. This place was hooked to all the other houses in a long row and had no yard, either back or front. There were four rooms. Her brother and she shared one of those rooms, while her stepfather and mother shared another.

There was a kitchen and living room of sorts, and the evenings at the kitchen table found her reciting her times tables over and over again. He would drill them and drill them, until she had them perfect. One times one is one, one times two is two, and ad nauseum to twelve times twelve is one hundred and forty-four. That's probably why she could still remember them, anyone who repeats them that many times, unless they are a bumbling idiot, is bound to remember them.

Sam had four brothers and they were all in the construction business so naturally times with them were full of work-related talk and congenial drinking. Sometimes the drinking would get a little too congenial and the talking would become heated, especially if her mother were involved.

Veronica was too beautiful to believe, like a movie star that had decided not to be on stage but to spend her time playing a role of wife and mother. Oftentimes her beauty brought problems, as Sam would see her friendly eyes and behold the effect they had on others when they would be socializing, and then later in the quiet of the night Marissa would be awakened by heated voices, arguments, and fights. She remembered one such night when she was perhaps 10 or 11, rising in the morning to find a frying pan sticking out of the wall. She could only wonder at how it got there, but when her mother saw her looking at it, she declared that she had thrown it at her stepfather because of his abusive attitude. She hated to see those things and those fights and, even now, finds herself unwilling to enter into confrontations, even when she knows she's in the right. It would be much later that she would be drawn into the confrontations with them, but for now all she was big enough to do was stand and listen to the sobs of her mother and the ranting of her stepfather. She had never heard a man raise his voice to a woman before; her grandpa was unfailingly kind and courteous to her grandma. What did it mean?

But except for the occasional dash away to teach him a lesson, her mother stuck to him, and life bumbled along. The only fly in the ointment was her brother Ryan. Sam did not like him; it was apparent even to her as young as she was, and so her mother rushed to defend him even more. Poor Ryan; she, too, would take his part and protect him.

Sam would come in from work and find some silly thing left undone or some chore outside that should have been done, and thrash around the house throwing this and that every which way. Her mother and she would roll their eyes and look at each other or the ceiling waiting for the tempest to be over and the interrogation to begin. Who had left the hoses lying around? Why wasn't the lawn finished? Where was Ryan? All the interrogations would always finish with "Where is Ryan?"

Couldn't anyone pick up, put away, but him? Of course we could but he would always see the times we had been called away to something for mother or distracted by a neighbor or interrupted by a phone call and so, of course, the things would be as he found them and the furies would begin. By the time Marissa was in her late adolescence, she began to police the outside before he would arrive to try and ward off the furies. When HIS son was born, of course, the mess became acceptable, for you couldn't expect an infant to pick up; it was their job to scatter things around.

Nevertheless, the days when Ryan was still at home were strained and they both longed to be away from the incessant arguments and fights.

November 1837

Her mamma was wrong; she never did get used to missing her. The school was cold and damp and the lessons were never-ending. The other girls looked down on her and asked her questions she couldn't answer. Who were her mother and father? Where had she come from? All those things that she wondered about herself, but couldn't find the answers to. Summer could not come too soon for her.

She would write in her journal, long poems filled with the longings and memories of her country home with Mamma. She was growing more and more introspective as the years went by, it was only on those holidays at the cottage, seated before the fire, that she was outgoing and sparkling, matching the snap and crackle of the flames, while she recounted the school stories to Matilda.

September 1954

During those days Marissa met the friends she would have for a lifetime, girls that shaped her thinking and her habits. They were a close group, chatty and friendly, always willing to help and share. There was Wilma who lived on the street behind her house and had this great older brother Fred. Wilma had the most beautiful skin of anyone she had ever seen and Ryan said it was so pretty it looked "blue."

Then there was Alicia who lived over the hill in a housing project somewhat like the one Marissa lived in, where all the houses looked the same. Alicia was one of six children and her mother was a dancer. Alicia and her brothers and sisters learned to tap dance and do ballet. Alicia was very graceful with the most startling blue eyes and loveliest widow's peak Marissa had ever seen.

Next came Helen, the sister of one of the most sought-after boys in school. Helen was small and dark and completely captivating. She was the most vivacious in the group and she and her grade school boyfriend and sweetheart provided the first look at true love in the making.

Lastly, there was Elaine, so much the Irish colleen, Marissa felt a kinship with her from the start. Elaine lived a mile or two away, but was on her school route, and so they visited back and forth on the way to school and during lunchtime breaks. It would be Elaine who would listen to her yearn for a high school sweetheart or suffer over the possibility of a breakup in the family that she felt was only held together by a thread.

A year or so later, Jeannetta came into the group having moved from another district when her parents were transferred into the area. Jeannetta was the blonde mysterious stranger to many, but they welcomed her.

Finally, there was Marissa, blue eyed with soft brown hair and a slightly melancholy air about her, perhaps even a dreamy quality to her demeanor. The six of them were together as much as six people can be, and, what one couldn't think of the other five would. Ryan would be entranced by her friends, having a crush on first one and then another of them. Oh, if he had only married one of them, how different his life might have been. But that is a different story.

During these days her time was pretty much her own and she was free most evenings to visit on the phone with her friends, have them over for chats, or go to their homes for the same. It wasn't until the next year her time began to be very busy. Marissa remembered vividly the day she heard the news. Her mother called her from her room to tell her she was going to have another baby. Marissa was thirteen years old and had just finished grade school. The next year she and all of her friends would start to junior high school. She didn't think anything about how having a new baby brother or baby sister would change her life; after all, it was her mother who was having the baby, right? Right! Wrong! The day her brother, Richard, was born was the day her whole world began to change. She loved him from the first; he was so small and defenseless. She would help her mother change and feed him and do more and more of the household chores. Veronica did not regain her health quickly after he was born, and needed much more assistance than she did before. Perhaps this is what happens when you have a baby late in life, perhaps everything breaks down sooner. As Marissa became more capable in caring for her brother, her mother leaned more heavily on her. She knew then that motherhood was something she could look forward to.

While Richard was still small, she would climb into his crib with him and sing him to sleep. Sometimes it almost felt like he was her child but he wasn't. Just her brother to care for, and care for him, she did. There wasn't as much time to talk on the phone with her friends as before but that was okay. She would visit at school and on the ride to and from school as before, and if they didn't do as many overnight things, they did get together from time to time at parties.

Marissa never felt that she was missing anything then, she was always too busy with Richard. It was like having a real live doll to play with. And he was a lovable, if somewhat spoiled little boy. He had his father's and mother's dark hair and dark eyes, and most times carried a smile on his face. It was only when his will was thwarted that he could be defiant. But she was a match for him and determined not to let him become too unruly. Mother would allow him the freedoms that Sam indulged, and sometimes she could see Ryan watching with hurtful eyes at the familiarity and softness that Richard would receive and which he had always looked for but never found from Sam. Perhaps it is why Marissa stepped between Sam and Ryan more and more as time went on. She seemed to be protected from the abuse from Sam while Ryan got his share and hers, too. Unfair as it was, she could do nothing but watch in anger and seethe at the unfairness. Life never seemed to be fair in those days. But as long as she kept her distance from Sam, she was able to mitigate some of the unfairness.

Turning a corner in life, though, Marissa started senior high school and she and her friends had more to chat about. The dates on Saturday night and the schoolgirl crushes, they had on this boy and that. Richard was now old enough for Veronica to handle and she had recovered much of her old stamina, so Marissa was only needed to baby-sit him on the nights when her mother and Sam would go out for an evening.

"Riinngg…riinnggg!" Marissa jumped to answer the telephone before someone else reached it.

"Hello, this is Marissa. Who's there?"

"Hi, this is Elaine, how is everything coming for the party?"

A Halloween party had been planned at Marissa's house, everyone was coming and it was important to plan and decorate the basement just right.

"We need to get together and see about gathering decorations for the party," Marissa said.

"When do you want to do it?"

"Well, it will have to be after dark, because we will have to sneak into the farmer's fields in the bottom land and get the pumpkins and cornstalks that we need."

"Are you sure that this is a good idea?" Elaine said.

"I can't afford to pay for all the decorations we need, can you?"

"No, but maybe we don't need that many."

"Maybe not, but the pumpkins are just rotting in the fields, no one is going to buy them after Halloween, and the cornstalks will just blow down and be chopped up, why shouldn't we get them, instead of letting them go to waste?" Marissa said rationalized, trying to make her petty theft ideas palatable to her friend.

"Okay, I'll get Alicia and we will be at your house on Friday night to go, don't let anyone know what we are doing, or we will be in big trouble."

"Don't worry, I know I will be in trouble if my stepfather finds out," Marissa said.

The leftover pumpkins littered the fields and shone in the moonlight, while the cornstalks rustled in the windy darkness as they drove along the top of the river levee. They couldn't find the way off and down into the fields. As Marissa drove, a line of trees loomed in front of the car, and without the lights on they couldn't distinguish how far or near they were. There was nowhere to turn around and if she turned on the lights to see ahead, they would be seen driving somewhere they weren't supposed to be.

"Oh darn, now I will have to back off this thing," Marissa groaned.

"Marissa, be careful. I will watch out the back," Elaine said.

Slowly backing the car in the direction she had come, Marissa craned her neck to see in the darkness. Sure enough, the car started slipping ever so slowly off the side of the levee. Marissa pushed on the accelerator and found her car buried to the axles in the soft earth of the levee.

"Oh heck, how am I going to get this thing off of here now?"

"We're just going to have to go get help," Alicia said.

"Okay, you and I'll walk to the nearest lighted house and get help. Elaine, you stay here with the car," Marissa said.

"All right, but just remember I was against this from the start."

"I know, I know, and you were right, I should have listened to you," Marissa replied.

So leaving Elaine with the car, Alicia and Marissa started the walk across the dark fields toward the nearest light.

"Knock, knock," they tapped on the farmhouse door.

"Who's there?" a voice answered.

"Sir, we have stuck a car on the levee. Can you help us get out?" came the subdued reply.

"What the devil are you doing on the levee at this hour?"

Confessing to their intentions, the two girls stood shamefaced in front of the owner of the fields and faced his lecture.

"You know, you could have come and asked, perhaps you would have been given the things you wanted without all this sneaking around," he said.

"Yes sir, we feel badly about all of this. I'm sorry to be such a bother to you," Marissa said.

"Well, come on then, let me get my tractor, but see that you girls keep off the levee at night, it's not safe."

"Yes sir," they said.

They followed the farmer to where his tractor was parked, and then riding one on either side of him holding onto the tractor fenders, they made their way back to the car and Elaine. It was short work for the farmer to attach a length of chain to the back of the car and pull it off the levee. They left the area with the farmer still shaking his head at them and headed home.

"No pumpkins," Elaine said.

"No cornstalks," Alicia said.

"Don't rub it in," Marissa said.

The party, though, was decorated in style and charm with cornstalks tied to supporting beams in the basement and the occasional jack-o-lantern peeking around the bottom. Mother had come through again. And there standing in the middle of her basement floor was Jim, brother of her best friend and bigtime senior at school.

"Marissa, I hope you don't mind my just showing up at your party, Helen couldn't get here unless I brought her and Dad says I have to drive she and Keith back home, so here I am." Jim grinned at her sheepishly.

"No, of course, you can come too. Please enjoy yourself." Marissa blushed, smiling up at him.

She supposed Helen had put him up to it to get them together. She kept saying they belonged together. Marissa liked him and he was real nice, class president, super smart, and on the basketball team. A girl could do worse than have Jim Wiggins angling for her.

October 1841

"I have seen him again today, but Mamma says I must not encourage him, he is beneath my station. I don't understand what Mamma means. What station? But at least I am home for good now. Mamma is not well and I knows she needs me more than ever. There the tea is ready; I will just take it upstairs to her," Catherine mused to herself.

Knocking at the door, she heard her voice, "Is that you, Cathy?"

"Yes, Mamma, here I am with your tea."

"Such a sweet child you are, my dear, but come and sit beside me now while I take my tea. There are things I must discuss with you and I am afraid to wait. St. Peter may be calling me soon and I have information you need to have." Mamma patted beside her on the bed.

"What information?"

"Well, dear, you know I love you like my own, but you are not my own child. Many years ago, you were brought to me in the night, just a swaddling child, to care for and I have kept you all these years because I loved you. But surely you must have realized I could not have kept you at a private school for your education all these years and that the money must have come from somewhere."

"I know you are not my real mamma, but it doesn't matter. I love you as if you were and I always will."

"Yes, my child, I know you would, but I am reaching the end of the road and I must prepare you for that end. If something should happen to me, you must go to the gentleman whose name appears on a letter that I have secreted away in a hidden place in the hearth. Look under the fourth stone from the end and you will find a box buried under the dirt in that place. The gentleman will be of help to you and there is also a purse there to take care of my final expense and keep you until you make your way to the gentleman's residence. Now be a sweet thing and let me rest and no more questions tonight."

Cathy walked downstairs with the tea things and sat looking at the hearth, the same one her cradle had sat beside so many years ago and wondered what she would find under the stone. But she could not bring herself to open Pandora's box until her mamma was gone; best to let sleeping dogs lie.

Perhaps the man with the warm eyes would see her again. His eyes held great promise, but, of what, she was still unaware. She had promised her mamma that she would not meet him and she had not. She still didn't understand why she was not supposed to, but she would honor her promise.

CHAPTER THREE

November 1957

Two weeks went by and still no call from Stephen. What was going on, what had happened? Marissa saw him at school but it was as if he didn't want anyone to know he knew her. She knew he cared, or at least had thought he cared, but now he was so distant. It never occurred to her that he would doubt her feelings for him. Then on the Wednesday of the third week, the phone rang. It was Stephen. He wanted to see her again and could she go to a movie that weekend? Friday or Saturday night?

"Of course, I can," she blurted. "Either night is great with me, you decide."

Marissa hated herself for sounding so eager, but she had been so unhappy when he didn't call or talk with her in school. Now that they were going to go out again, it was all right and all was forgiven. What a shock she would be in for!

Saturday night came and there was Stephen in the driveway to pick her up. Blowing the horn for her, she came pouring out the door like a waterfall looking for the spillway. Marissa was always punctual and couldn't understand why her mother was looking at her that way. Of course, she had to run, they would just have time to make the movie.

The evening was just as magical as before, with the same ending in her driveway, only this time Stephen was even more ardent and caressed her with burning hands. She couldn't stand it; she had to tell him how much she cared for him. Surely he cared for her otherwise; why else touch, hold, and kiss her this way?

"Stephen," Marissa said, "I love you, I know I do, even though we haven't spent that much time together, I know I will always feel this way."

"Marissa," Stephen answered, "I hope you mean what you say, I don't want to be dumped like Jim was and I fear that you may treat me the same way."

Marissa was devastated. Didn't he realize that if it weren't for him, she would never have left Jim in the first place? The strength of the emotions she felt for him had caused her to act in the way she did. She had been powerless against the tide of longing for him that had swept over her. He didn't trust her and didn't want to be humiliated and that was why he treated her the way he did at school! He didn't want anyone to know that they were dating. Okay, that meant that she would just have to prove to him that she meant what she said.

She set out to prove him wrong. She would show him how much she loved him. She could wait forever for him, if necessary. They continued to date that year while Stephen was still a senior. After he graduated and was no longer at school, Marissa kept herself only for him, but the pressure of the lovemaking that was kept at bay began to show itself in Stephen and he begged her to give herself body and soul to him. She insisted that she wanted to wait for her wedding night to give herself to him and couldn't he understand that, didn't he love her enough to wait for her? The fights began; the pressures too great to bear began to separate Stephen from her.

She suffered in his absence and then that summer, Stephen took a job out of town and was truly separated from her. She would write to him and pour out her feelings in the letters that winged their way to him. Still she waited for him. Would he never come home? Would they never be happy together?

He returned to her that fall and they picked up where they had left off. Marissa had always wanted Stephen to take her to her senior prom and when the time drew near, she asked him to escort her. He agreed, but three weeks before the prom was to occur, they had a terrible fight over the sex issue and Stephen didn't call.

Marissa was angry, it wasn't fair, she had waited and saved herself for him, couldn't he at least be able to wait as well? She didn't realize the pain and suffering he was going through while she asked him to wait. He wanted her, so much so that he would go home aching and in pain. She couldn't know this, innocent as she was, she couldn't understand. Now she was stood up for her own senior prom. "I'll find someone else to take me to the prom if that is the way he was going to be. But who?" she mused. She hadn't been seeing anyone else since she had started seeing Stephen, who could she ask? Then she remembered, Jim had said that he would always be her friend. Could she in good conscience ask Jim to be her escort? She would do it. She would show Stephen that he couldn't treat her this way.

She called Jim. "Jim, I know this is kind of short notice, but I don't have a date to the senior prom and I wondered if you would like to escort me?"

"Yes, Marissa, I would love to take you," Jim accepted.

Two days before the prom, Stephen called, "Marissa, do you still want me to take you to the prom?" he asked. How dare he wait until the last minute to call her, she fumed to herself.

"No, you didn't need to bother, I've found someone else to take me, thank you very much," Marissa replied in the coldest voice she could muster. She would show him, she was sure that he had known about her asking Jim, he had just called to see if he could snatch her away again. She didn't care if she hurt him, he had hurt her many times in the last year. It seemed that all they did was unwillingly hurt the other. But no more, she would get on with life and Stephen had shown that he could do very well without her.

The night of prom came and everyone was looking special with their corsages and long gowns. The gymnasium was decorated with hanging fishnet and soft lights, and Jim swept her into his arms to dance every dance, but Marissa's heart was not in the evening. It was a very unhappy affair for her, even though she smiled and danced and pretended to be very gay, she was crushed inside. Stephen hadn't cared enough to take her to the prom; he had picked a fight with her so he wouldn't have to be seen with her at the prom. Her very soul hurt, there was no magical place that night for her. Jim hoped that she had seen the light at last.

"Marissa, are things over between you and Stephen?"

"Yes, I am afraid they are now. I can't seem to feel that he really cares about me. Everytime I am with him, I know how I feel, but then he starts pressing me and I guess I get scared that he won't love me always and I pull back. But this time I really think we are quits."

"Do you think that we could see each other again?" Jim asked.

"Perhaps when we get back from Nebraska, maybe you can call me," Marissa replied.

"What is in Nebraska?" Jim asked.

"I have to go with my family there this summer, Sam is being transferred there this summer and the whole family has to go."

"I will get in touch with you when you get back," Jim said.

"Okay," Marissa whispered. Later she looked deep inside herself at the feelings she had for him, were they friendship only or could the old relationship be revived? Only time would tell.

At the end of the night, she vowed that she would never attend another affair just because it seemed the thing to do. Graduation found Marissa finished with her years in school, it was time to move out into the working world. She wanted to attend college but those opportunities were beyond her. When she got back from Nebraska, she would start to hunt for a job in earnest. And so she returned to find a job she liked and was good at. It was at a local manufacturing concern where her flying fingers were put to good use. Thank the heavens for taking that high school typing class.

January 1960

She started dating several different men, she had even tried seeing Jim again, but no one had touched her heart since Stephen. Work was keeping her mind occupied and her days filled, plus the feeling of having her own income now and some degree of independence helped. Even though she still lived at home, her days and nights were her own without curfews and watchful eyes to check on every movement. Sam seemed content to let her do her own thing as long as she kept her nose clean. She still kept her distance from him, though, and watched as the troubles began to brew between him and her mother.

One particular evening more than a year after she and Stephen had broken up, she and some of her friends had gone to a local nightclub to dance. She was enjoying herself, joking and laughing with everyone, when in walked Stephen with another guy. She was so surprised that she could hardly speak. Why was Stephen here? He never came here. She was even more surprised when he walked up to her and asked if he could take her home. What did he want after all this time? He looked like he had been drinking. Was he drunk? Perhaps a little, she had better let him take her home, then she could see if he could drive all right. Why, she wondered, did she care? It had been over a year since she had seen or heard from him. What did he want now? Well, she would find out on the way home.

"Marissa," Stephen mumbled, "perhaps you should drive us, I think I may have had a little too much to drink. I'm okay, just need a little air."

"All right, Stephen, but how is your friend getting home or is he coming too?" Marissa answered. Stephen walked to his friend and after a hurried conversation, returned to Marissa.

"It's alright, he's got a ride." Stephen winked as he climbed into the car with her. It was unusual that she had not driven herself there that night, but she had lent her car to a friend and was hitching a ride herself. It was like de ja vous, almost like the beginning of their roller coaster relationship. Only this time she was in control of herself. She was in the driver's seat in more ways than one.

It was a short distance from the nightclub to her house and Marissa couldn't help wondering what was coming next. She pulled the car into her driveway and started to open the door to get out when Stephen grabbed her arm to stop her.

"Marissa, we need to talk. I have something to say. I have decided that we should get engaged and both work our jobs for a year and then get married. What do you think about that?"

Marissa was dumbfounded. She had not heard a word from this man for a year. She hadn't even seen his face either for all that time and here he was telling her that HE had decided that they should get engaged, save their money, and after another year get married.

This was the man she had worshipped for three years or more. She had practically groveled to get to see him and now here he was planning her life for her as if they had just seen each other yesterday. Who did he think he was? She was never so angry in her life. Half drunk and proposing to her. He would probably forget all about it in the morning, just like the prom, or maybe he thought the only way to get her into bed was to propose, and she would just fall all over him. Her anger spilled over him in a torrent of words.

"Stephen, if you had asked me this when I was a senior in high school, I would have quit school and married you, but you let me wait just a little too long. You let me sit on the shelf while you did your thing just a little too long and now I find that there are things that I NEED to do. Things like getting my own apartment and making my own decisions and standing on my own two feet. So I have to say, I am just not ready now," Marissa answered.

He looked at her for a long moment and then replied, "I guess I always thought when I was ready, you'd be ready," Stephen said in the softest voice she had ever heard him use.

The anger inside her now congealed into a hard cold stone which lay in the pit of her stomach. "Yes, I know, you took me for granted. But you took me for granted just a little too long."

She jumped from the car and ran to the house. Her anger was still boiling as she threw herself down on her bed. Finally, the anger subsided and the tears began to flow. Why had he not wanted her before? Why wait until he was half drunk to ask her? Didn't he want her to believe in him? She would show him, she would move into an apartment and stand on her own two feet.

Perhaps it was herself she doubted. Perhaps it was she and a long-term relationship with Stephen she feared. After seeing the second marriage of her mother, perhaps she didn't feel she could handle the confrontations and fights which seemed to be inevitable in these kinds of emotional relationships. She just didn't know anymore. She knew that until she knew herself, she wouldn't be able to commit to anyone.

February 1843

Cathy was beside herself with grief; her mamma, her beloved mamma, was gone. How could it be? She had cared for her for the past two years, and now at almost nineteen years old she was alone. More alone than she had ever been in her life. The priest had come and counseled her about the funeral arrangements and she knew that she must begin the preparations, but she felt so unsure and leaden as though every effort were sapping the last ounce of strength she had left.

There, at the door, she thought she heard a gentle rapping. Yes, she was sure, someone was rapping at the door. She struggled to rise from the chair and crossed to the door. When she opened it inward to the room, she saw, standing on the porch, the man of the village with the smoldering eyes.

"Sir, pray tell me who you are inquiring for?"

"I know there is only you here now, Cathy, so it must be you I am seeking."

"And your name, sir, since we have not been introduced before."

"Daniel," he replied, "Daniel Graves."

"Sir, my mamma has just been taken from me and I haven't quite my wits about me, what is it you are here for?"

"I am here to be of service, miss, I can help you with the arrangements, as I knew your mamma, though she kept you far from me."

"How is it you knew my mamma?"

"My father is the rental agent for your mamma's house and I was often present when she came to pay her yearly rental on the cottage."

"Oh, I had no idea that this house was yours. Please do not worry, I will be leaving as soon after the funeral that I can get my things together."

"Oh, please don't be alarmed, I didn't mean to worry you about it, you may stay as long as you like. Only please let me be of assistance in this time of grief for you."

"Thank you for your kindness, and yes, since you knew my mamma's history you would also know of any relatives I should notify. For all the years I spent with her, there was only one man who ever came to see us and the last visit was long ago, so I guess he no longer cares."

"Don't worry your lovely head about it, I will inquire and also make the arrangements for the funeral and internment. And now I will take my leave until the morrow." Daniel gathered his coat and removed himself from her presence.

Mamma, why didn't you want me to meet him? He seems pleasant and eager to help. I can not but wonder that you wouldn't want me to meet someone who would be interested in my welfare, she wondered as she watched him down the path to the road.

The day dawned gray and mist-shrouded and it fit Cathy's mood exactly. She would miss her mamma terribly. The churchyard was filled with many people, mostly there to say goodbye, but some to catch a look at the young miss who was now alone and helpless. The priest led the procession with his book of prayers followed by the six strong men who had volunteered to carry her mamma to her final resting place, and behind, alone and covered head to toe in black, came the young miss. A black parasol covering her head from the mist, she walked slowly and unwaveringly behind the box in front. Stepping out of the crowd to walk beside her, came Daniel of the night before to offer her his arm and strength.

At last the words were said, the box was lowered, and as she rose to toss the handful of earth upon the bier of her mamma, her strength failed her, she swooned into the arms of Daniel standing next to her.

She awoke hearing the rustling of someone filling the kettle and stirring the fire up at the hearth. She was back in her own house, lying in her own bed. How had she arrived there? And then she heard him on the stairs.

"Sir, what has happened? How did I arrive here in my bed? Pray tell me what is amiss."

"Nothing is amiss, Cathy, you merely swooned and I carried you back here and put you to bed. Are you feeling better now? Would you like some tea?" And Cathy could see a tea tray in his hands as he stood before her.

"Yes, thank you very much, how silly of me to swoon. I never swoon. It must have been some vapor in the air." In truth she did feel weak and could not remember when she had last supped. The tea tray looked inviting and she drew herself up from the bed to join him by the fire.

"You are too kind to care for me in this way, I must repay you some way."

At that remark, his head jerked up and a slow smile lit his face. But then he saw that she indeed did mean what she had said and she was not a trollop that he could dally with.

"Nonsense, nothing you wouldn't have done for me if the situations were reversed. Think nothing more about it," he protested.

Then she turned her face to his with a winning smile that threatened to dwarf the sun in its glory and he was lost. He was completely captivated by her and tried in every way he could to show her his devotion. But she was still distracted by her mamma's death and so after assuring himself that it was safe to leave her, he took himself off.

Cathy sat before the fire remembering the conversations she had had with her mamma and the tears slowly welled into her eyes. It was quiet in the house, too quiet, and she couldn't just sit here crying her eyes red. She must be about something, and she remembered the hearthstone and the box. Now which side had her mamma said it was under? She lifted stone after stone and dug down and finally under the fourth stone she found the place and the box. She pulled it from the dirt and swept the top clean as she sat it on the tea table. She would have to get something to pry it open, it had rusted with age.

She crossed to the drawer in the desk and took a letter opener out and started to work on the lid of the box. Gradually as she pried and pried, it came loose and the contents of the box were revealed. Inside was a letter addressed to a Mr. Joseph Lawson, Barrister, 27 Downing Street, London, England. There also on the bottom of the box lay the purse that she had seen the man give her mamma all those years ago.

Tomorrow she would ready herself to go to London, but first she must put the house in order, as she knew she wouldn't be returning to it again.

The next day as Cathy was readying herself for the journey to London, she began to put her house in order. What would she find on her arrival in London? Whatever it was, she must be prepared for it. She began her search with her mamma's desk where she had worked for the last three years keeping the household accounts. It was here that she had sat and written the poetry that had entertained her mamma with its lyrical musical cadence. She looked through the papers and found the binder, which she had stored the poems in. Some of them were good, she knew that, but most were early works of a fertile imagination and the yearnings of a young heart. Perhaps someone might find them interesting, she would be sure and pack them in her valise. She laid the folder on the table with the letter to the barrister on top and went upstairs to gather her clothing. She would have to find a porter to take her things to the hostelry where she might find transport to London.

Again, she heard the door being tapped and hurried downstairs to open it. There was Daniel standing as before on the stoop about to rap again. He looked beyond her to the valise and asked, "Are you going somewhere? Perhaps I can be of assistance again."

"You have been so kind, I don't like to constantly be requiring you to clear the way for me. It seems I must travel to London. How might that be accomplished?"

"It would be my pleasure to send you in my coach if you would permit me. I would accompany you myself but I have pressing business here at the moment."

"That is too much, I can not repay you for this kindness now, but be sure someday I will."

"Cathy, I wish you didn't have to go; you don't you know, you could stay here and continue in your mamma's house. I would never put you out. You know that, don't you?"

"Daniel, I feel that I must go to London, it was my mamma's wish that I contact someone and until I do I cannot plan a life. Please don't try to make me stay, I will return as soon as I can."

"That is all that I ask, Cathy, that you come back and let us become better friends. Perhaps someday more than friends. I'll wait for your return."

Daniel left and was as good as his word, when the next morning a carriage arrived at the door of the house to collect Miss Catherine Aurora Barrett. She stepped into the coach and the driver whisked his whip and with a jerk of the reins the matched pair of horses stepped lively and pulled the coach away. It was many hours later when they arrived on the outskirts of London. The coachman slowed the coach to a stop and came down to speak to Cathy.

"Miss, where am I to carry you if I may ask?" the coachman inquired.

"I need to find a hotel, but first I must go to see the gentleman at this address," and she showed him the letter that she had.

"I know this street, miss. I can have you there before they close the doors for the night." He jumped back aboard his seat and snapped the whip again and they went rocketing down the London streets.

They soon arrived at the front of a large imposing building and Cathy looked at the front where a brass plague, displayed for all to see, gave the name of Joseph Lawson, Barrister. Cathy opened the door of the coach and asked the driver if he could wait while she met with the barrister and then help her find a good small hotel.

She climbed the steps of the building and pulled the bell at the door. A small man dressed in suit and tie with eyeglasses pushed up on his forehead opened the door and bade her enter. When she inquired for Mr. Lawson, she was asked her business and upon presenting the letter she had been given, she was motioned to a chair to wait. She didn't have long to wait. In a matter of minutes, the barrister himself came out to meet her.

"Miss Catherine, please come in, come in. I have just finished reading the letter you have brought with you and I am delighted to meet you." The man was very polite to her and extremely apologetic. "I am sorry you have had such a long journey. Have you had supper or any sort of refreshment since you started out?"

She declared that she had not and perhaps a cup of tea would be welcome. The barrister sent his assistant to fetch that for her and directed her to his office. There settled in a wingback chair in front of the fire, she waited for the man to continue. What was in the letter that she had carried? Why was he so apologetic and nice to her?

"Mr. Lawson, I have no idea what was in the letter which I carried to you, but I was required by my mamma to bear it to you after her death. I confess that I am curious why I am here so please do not keep me in suspense about the matter. What was in the letter?"

"Catherine, I must admit I don't know quite how to explain this to you, but the letter contained instructions to me in regards to you after your mamma's death and they are particular in the extreme. It seems that you are the inheritor of quite a large sum of money but you can only get it under certain conditions. These conditions are, that upon receiving this money, you are to sever all ties to this country and those abiding here and make your residence in the Americas."

"Why must I go to the Americas? What is there that compels me to go?"

"Well, for one thing the money which I spoke of is there, residing in financial institutions awaiting your letters of introduction. I am having those prepared as we speak. They will introduce you to a barrister in New York who will be of immense help to you in securing what is rightfully yours."

"Where did these moneys come from?"

"Well, a long time ago your grandfather came to me and set up a trust for you, in the event that you survived infancy, and left my father in charge of the matter. Since my father has gone to his rewards, it is left to me to administer it for you."

"Who was my grandfather and why didn't I live with him? I know my mother is dead. So why didn't I live with my grandfather?"

"Your mother is not dead, but your grandfather did not want the disgrace of a child born out of wedlock to blemish her name or the family name and so you were separated from her after birth. She nearly died of the birth and the sorrow of your separation, but he was adamant about your removal and so she agreed as long as you would be taken care of."

"And so he took me and left me with Mamma. What a hateful man! I am glad I did not live with him now. He would have made my life terrible. I can just barely remember him with his dark looks coming to our house and staring at me," Catherine said bitterly, remembering the man who would intrude on the solitude of the cottage.

"Well, miss, what is it to be? Will you claim your fortune in the Americas? You are a grown woman now and your mother would not know you if she saw you on the street. What will it be?" he asked.

"Must I go at once?"

"Yes, as soon as I can book passage on a ship."

"Then let it be as you have said, there is nothing left here now that Mamma is gone, I might as well as go to the Americas as anywhere." Cathy paused a moment and then asked, "Can you recommend a good hotel, I came straight here and I do not have accommodations."

"By all means, there is a good hotel just around the square from this office and it will be convenient for us to meet on the morrow for there are many papers for you to sign and I can tell that you need to rest for now. I will see you to your coach and then we will get together tomorrow."

"Forgive me, if I have seemed uncharitable, but it is so much to take in. Did the paper say nothing about my father at all then?"

"No, my dear, your mother never divulged his name I'm afraid," Lawson replied.

"Well, then, as there is no one who wants me here, I will go."

With instructions to the coachman on where to take her, Lawson bid Cathy good evening and she departed from his office. Tomorrow would see the beginning of a new life for her. She hoped there would be no surprises in the Americas like the one she had today.

CHAPTER FOUR

January 1962

It was moving day. Marissa was packing all the things she supposed she would need in the new apartment. It was in the city and she would be sharing expenses with two nurses and one female CPA so it seemed her expenses would be do-able. It was exciting to be on her own learning all the ins and outs of the city. She could come and go as she pleased. It was going to be wonderful, and it was. The other girls worked different shifts and so Marissa did not see as much of her roommates as she thought she would. For her part that was okay, she had a busy work life and an active social one.

Her friend, Alicia, lived in the city also and they did the nightclub circuit in the Italian part of town. It seemed the safest place for young women without escorts. There was one young Italian man who took a fancy to Marissa and she found him amusing and entertaining and liked his family, though her romantic feelings were still tucked safely inside. No more men for our Marissa. No more broken dates and fights over sex. No sir, she was on her own and not willing to give her heart again.

Marissa's brother joined her many nights at the nightclubs to dance and she and Ryan made a fancy-stepping couple on the dance floor. Ryan confided to her, though, that their mother was not doing too well in the financial department and their stepfather was working full time out of town. It looked as though the marriage was not going to hold together after all. He felt sorry for Richard, poor kid was only six now and really didn't understand all the undercurrents going on in the family. But he was a bright kid, not going to be too long before he figured it all out.

"Ryan," Marissa said, "are you telling me this to get me to move back home? Does Mom need me to? I can, you know, if she needs the money. I could just as easily pay Mom the money I use for the apartment. If she wants me to, all she has to do is tell me."

"Marissa," Ryan replied, "you have to do what you have to do. Although, yes, I think the money would help, because I am not working yet, and it is pretty tight at home. You know Mom, though, she will never ask you to, you will have to suggest it or something, like it will help you more than her."

"Well, don't say anything to Mom yet. I have to give notice to my roommates and see if they can get someone to take over my part of the lease. I have been there for six months and I need to get someone to move in and not let them down," Marissa said.

"I won't, but if you are going to do it, don't wait too long to mention it to Mom, I think she is looking to move herself if she doesn't get help," Ryan muttered. "Sam isn't sending her any money for the house or for Richard."

"I can't believe he would just desert Richard. I can see him letting Mom suffer, he has been real good at that, but Richard, that goes out of character, even for him. But okay," Marissa said, "just give me a few days to get with the girls."

Marissa went home that night and waited up until her roommates got off their shifts to talk with them. They said not to worry about it, they were sure that they could get someone to move in and help split expenses from the nursing school. They understood the reasons behind her moving home.

And so one early summer evening in June, Marissa drove back home to live with her mother and two brothers again. It was different coming back home after being on her own. Marissa began to think again about what she had said to Stephen. She didn't know how to win him back, or whether she even could. She seemed to be comparing everyone she met with him. She was still uncertain whether he had ever really loved her, even though he had asked her to marry. Stephen never really said the words that she wanted to hear. He had never really shown her he loved her as she needed to be loved and perhaps that was the whole problem. Marissa needed to be loved completely and without reservation. She needed someone to be her soul mate, someone who would empathize with her and encourage her.

As she was emptying boxes and organizing her closets and drawers, there was someone ringing the doorbell!

Marissa fantasized that it was Stephen, that he had heard that she had come home and was waiting to tell her how much he had missed her and how much he loved her. Had someone told him she was moving home? Had her brother told him? She ran to answer the door, and flung it open only to see a different person standing there.

It was Donald Feinstein. She had danced with him one night at a club that she had been frequenting. He was nice enough and had asked her out but she had declined. She didn't know how he had found out where her mother lived and that she had moved back home. But there he was standing on the doorstep asking to come in.

Donald Feinstein was a car salesman, a used car salesman to boot, and having no experience whatsoever with salesmen, Marissa did not realize what she was starting by inviting him in to the living room. He was friendly, helpful, and outgoing with her mother and brother. He was charming and asked her out to dinner for the next evening. Marissa accepted his invitation as an interesting evening, but after one date, she decided maybe she would just be busy the next time he called. He didn't call! He just showed up again, and would not take "no" for an answer. Since Marissa did not have plans, she was swept into whatever ideas he came up with. There was a picnic and swim party at a local beach, dining and dancing in the evenings, playing cards with Mom and brother Ryan, and taking brother Richard to the zoo. He was all things to all people and he was determined to have Marissa as his own.

It was July and fast approaching Marissa's twenty-first birthday. One afternoon while Donald and Marissa were out driving they stopped at a drugstore to pick up a prescription for Marissa's mother.

While waiting, Donald maneuvered Marissa to the jewelry counter to look at jewelry. He would point out first one set of rings and then another, always asking Marissa which one she liked the best. Marissa was content to just look and finally to keep him quiet, she said, "Yes, perhaps that one was the best of the lot." On the way home with the medicine, Donald asked Marissa why she wasn't married, a pretty girl like herself.

"No marriage for me, at least not yet. I'm too young."

"We will be married by September, I make you a bet on that."

"Oh ho, you think so, do you? Well, I will take that bet, because I have no intention of marrying you or anyone else right now."

But within the week, the very ring set that Marissa had favored was purchased and tendered for her inspection and approval, and, by gosh, within the month they were engaged. What had happened to her decision to stay single? Why was she so pressured into giving her hand to this man? What did he say that convinced her to do it?

He was helpful to her in a time of need that no one else had shown. Her family was divorcing again and her mother needed all the help she could get.

Her brothers were without male images and she saw Donald as the savior and helper he might be.

Still though she had her doubts and paid a visit to see her father one night to ask him if the marriage was a wise decision. She was having misgivings and she was questioning how she felt about Donald. Her father said she must make her own decision, that he could not advise her, and so she took the easy path.

So before the end of September, they were married and Marissa lost her bet and virginity on the same night. Did Marissa live happily ever after? Alas, that was not to be. She would live to regret this hasty marriage.

She was a beautiful bride and was filled with hopes for the future; so for now she was spared the look into the future that might have shattered her happiness in the moment. Her friend, Alicia, was her maid of honor and, with her father on her arm, she approached the altar to see Donald waiting for her. He was as different from Stephen as night was from day. He was cocky, suave, and completely worldly, exuding confidence and control. That seemed to be a good trait to Marissa, but it was to become a serious character flaw that would threaten to destroy her in the future. "Now why did I think of Stephen when I saw Donald?" She put the thoughts from her head and walked toward him.

"Do you take this man to be your lawfully wedded husband?"

"I do," she said.

As she said her vows, her voice was soft and almost nonexistent, as though she could hardly get them out. Where was the feeling of ecstasy that she had experienced with Stephen? Perhaps after the wedding was over and they were relaxed and on their way to their honeymoon, those feelings would emerge. Surely, there was more to life than just excited feelings, wasn't there? This man had promised to love, cherish, and honor her, why didn't she feel safe? She asked these questions in her mind.

"Do you take this woman to be your lawfully wedded wife?"

"I do," he said.

"I now pronounce you man and wife."

The words rang with finality, her dreams of life with Stephen were over. She would never be the same person again. Would this man who wanted her prove to be the one who would keep her from dreaming and hurting over Stephen? Yes, she was determined to put him from her heart and mind. She would do it. She could do it.

March 1, 1843

The day dawned cool and the early morning fog still lingered around the corners of the buildings hugging the ground and swirling in the aftermath of the carriage wheels as coaches passed back and forth on the cobblestone street in front of her hotel. Cathy took morning tea at her table in her room beside the window and watched as first one and then another cloak-wrapped person passed on the street below. She wondered at the errands that took each one out on a cool morning such as this, but then remembered that she too would have to leave the warmth of the fire and go abroad to the barrister's office again today.

She would have to send word to Daniel that she would not be returning to the house he owned and that, indeed, she would be leaving the continent altogether. The reasons must be of necessity, be kept hidden, for she certainly did not want to advertise the circumstances of her birth. In this despondent frame of mind she picked up her pen and began to write.

My Dear Daniel,

I hope I may call you that for indeed in a very short time your kindnesses have endeared you to me. I can only tell you that it is with heavy heart that I take my leave from you and make a journey that is necessary for my welfare.

Please remember me with fondness as I will you and know that you are the one bright light that has shown for me during all this time of heavy sad darkness.

The poem that I enclose states my feelings at the moment and I hope helps to convey them to you.

Affectionately yours,
Catherine Aurora Barrett

On another piece of paper and penned in her hand were the following verses.

My Soul

If life will pass me by
I will not die.
If all my dreams should fly
I will not die.

And if sadness should envelop me
You must consider it just a passing phase
And if the sun refuses to shine on me
Just consider it another cloudy day.

If all my friends (if I have any)
Should forget me
I know I will not die.

For my feelings have been scarred,
They have hardened
And now they start to betray me
My soul might start to decay
So I wish you'd think no bad of me
For I'm remembering yesterday.

She folded both pieces of paper and secured them in an envelope, then addressing them to Daniel at her mamma's home, she called a porter and had them posted. She was sure that the post would be sent to him now that no one lived at the house anymore. She hoped he would understand, but there was no way she could tell him more.

Now to attend to the unpleasant lawyer things and be on her way. There was no use wishing for a visit with her mother. That door was closed to her forever and her father would never be shared with her. The best face she could put on it would be to leave this place and this land and strike out in the United States. She could do it, she knew she could. She would do it and take her dreams to another place and another time.

October, 1962

The honeymoon was in Chicago, and Chicago in October is not the most pleasant place to honeymoon, but even in the blustery cold, she was young and hopeful and saw the place as through rose-colored eyes. There were walks along the shore drive looking at the lake, bundled in sweaters and warm trousers, and lazy afternoons in the museums and art galleries wandering among the exhibits and paintings. Perhaps her misgivings had been a figment of her mind; perhaps everything would be all right after all. It was a short honeymoon and on returning they rented a mobile home and started housekeeping. On the very first night home, Donald began to set the pace of their married life. She would be left waiting for his return, supper most often burned or dried out beyond repair because he would neglect to call and say, "I'll be late this evening, dear."

Still Marissa strived to maintain a loving home. Donald had been generous in the days of their courting, but now that they were married the income was spent in other ways and the bills began to pile. When they could no longer afford the mobile home that he had provided, they were forced to move to her mother's house and resume their married life. This was to prove disastrous for all, as all the congeniality that Donald had heretofore shown to Mom and her brothers disappeared.

To keep the peace and still maintain good relations with her mother and brothers, Marissa looked for other housing. By now, it was apparent to all that she was no longer the sun around with Donald rotated. She began to long for a child to fill her empty life, since she was so often alone. She was to be cut off from her friends; Donald wanted her in their home not meandering around with her single friends. That would soon be made abundantly clear. Donald wanted to be the only child in that family and so, month in and month out, there was no child.

Until finally one June when they had been married two years, they took a vacation with Donald's parents, and he forgot himself, even though she had stopped using contraceptives, and Willow was conceived.

Marissa bloomed with good health most of the time during her pregnancy with Willow. Needing to share her feelings of joy with someone, she went on a visit one evening to one of her old friends. She and Elaine talked until the late hours of the night, and although she knew she should call Donald, she didn't. She wanted him to experience what it felt like to wonder where she was or what had happened to her as she so often did about him.

She arrived home that night to find an irate husband who accused her of every trick in the book. She should have been smart enough then to realize that he was only accusing her of what he was doing himself. He slapped her viciously, knocking her down and striking mortal terror in her for her expectant child. This was what she had seen her mother endure in her marriage to Sam. This is what had kept her from saying yes to Stephen all those years ago, and this is what she had come to receive by finally letting Donald break down her defenses and marrying him. She ran for the bedroom, remembering the rifle, which stood in the corner. She knew she was not strong enough to protect herself if he continued to hit her. But he was too quick and grabbed the gun from her hands as she was swinging it around. Now she was horrified as he slapped and pushed her to the floor.

Finally, she sobbed uncontrollably and screamed for mercy, all the while trying to protect her stomach. He was done with her. He left her alone. He must have been drinking because with neither word of apology nor answer, he went to bed and to sleep.

She crept into the bathroom and sponged her face. She would get away from him. She had to get away from him. She stole into the living room to wait until she could hear his breathing change and knew that he was fast asleep. Then tiptoeing as quietly as she could, she got her car keys and purse off the dresser and let herself out of the house. It was a short drive to her parents' home.

"Mother, help me," she sobbed, "I think he will kill me if I go back."

"What happened, what do you mean?" Her mother's concern registered in her questions.

"I stayed at Elaine's talking until midnight, and when I got home, he slapped me and knocked me down when I walked in the back door."

"Are you all right, did he hurt you seriously?"

"I think I am all right, but I pray nothing happens to the baby. He didn't seem to care whether I was pregnant or not, when he hit me."

"Stay here with us," her mother said. "I will see that you aren't bothered. You need a little time apart before you decide what you want to do."

She would not go back, nothing would induce her to go back.

A week later he came for her. He came for her at her mother's, contrite, sorry for all that had transpired. "Please, please, give me another chance," he cried. "What about our baby?" he extolled. Marissa had consulted an attorney; she could not divorce while she was pregnant. Perhaps he would be different now; perhaps he would change for the sake of the child.

So she went back home and, for the most part, had an uneventful pregnancy. Except for one episode with kidney infection, she managed to bring forth a beautiful baby girl with a minimum of effort and pain. He managed to keep his anger at bay and she kept herself in her home, all the time becoming more and more isolated. Only now there was Willow.

Willow, for her first four months of life, was a delight, smiling, cooing, and bubbling over. Marissa had a reason for living. Her life with Donald was deteriorating, his job changes were becoming ever more frequent and he was more and more involved with the drinking and bar hopping than ever. There were the excuses, he couldn't sell anymore, he was going into a new business, and he was depressed. There was always a reason.

When Willow was five months old, the sicknesses began. The recurring bladder and kidney infections that would send the child into crying, screaming fevers and Marissa and her mother scurrying to the doctors and hospitals that could not seem to help.

Donald had no patience for crying sick babies and found many reasons to be somewhere else during all this time. Poor man, how it must have belabored him to have to be in the same house with a sobbing infant. But there were doctors to see the child and medicines which would help for a while and surely when she was older these things would disappear, wouldn't they?

Finally, when Willow was sixteen months old, Marissa went back to work for a large publishing concern in the city that employed many typists. Now there would be regular money coming in and medical benefits.

Marissa kept at her job, leaning heavily on her mother and her new stepfather, Ronald, for help in watching Willow while she worked. Her mother had finally finished with Sam and some time later had married Ronald. Marissa liked him well enough and he was very supportive to her, helping in any way he could to keep Willow reasonably happy.

Like Marissa, Willow didn't see much of her father, he was always too busy to keep the child, and "wouldn't she be happier with her grandmother anyway," and so he pushed off the responsibility time after time. The days began to wind down to Willow's second birthday, in fact she was only two months away from it when the final blow to the marriage would occur.

Marissa had, for some time, suspected that Donald was seeing someone else but could never prove it. On their final evening as man and wife, she was endeavoring to get to the grocery to shop for the family. She was awaiting her husband's return so that she wouldn't have to bundle the child and take her out into the cold to shop. But he didn't come, and didn't come, so finally she called his office and was told that he always stopped at the local inn for drinks after work and would she like the number there. She replied, "Yes, she would," and promptly called him at the bar. After he told her "he would be there when he got there," she implored him to come home at once to take care of Willow. When he returned home, there was a terrible fight with the threat of more violence, and the decision that Willow and Marissa would be leaving the apartment that night.

Since he had no further regard for them than that, they did not need him either. They would return to the apartment after he had removed himself from it. He admitted that he was seeing someone else and that he didn't know if he wanted the marriage to continue but if she wanted to get help maybe it could.

Marissa broke down completely then, she was a failure, she had brought a child into the world whose father was self centered and uncaring, that she couldn't hold a husband, that she was not loving and caring herself.

Finally, that she was failure in taking care of her child and herself. After many sessions of counseling and talking it out, she came to realize that she had been avoiding the real problem, which was that she was afraid of caring too much and in essence had married a man whom she didn't really love and didn't want to return to. Once she accepted that it was as much her fault as his, she was able to move on and begin to build a life for herself and her child.

"Willow," Marissa whispered to her daughter, "we will be okay, honey. As long as we have each other, we will be okay. I love you, sweetheart, and Mama will never leave you."

"I love you, too, Mommy," Willow whispered back. "We be okay."

CHAPTER FIVE

February 1968

Almost a year later one cold February day, Marissa's mother was keeping the child for her while she worked. On this particularly busy day, the phone rang at work and her mother was on the other end of the receiver.

"Marissa," her mother said over the phone, "I think you better get home right away, Willow is really sick again." Marissa was busily typing on a manuscript from a new author that needed editing. It was not a good time to leave.

"Mom, did you call Dr. Bueller?" Marissa asked. "He can prescribe something."

"I called him, and he called me a hysterical grandmother," her mother answered. "You better come home and take her to see someone else, someone who will get to the bottom of this problem. Willow is almost three now and she shouldn't still be having these problems!"

"Okay, Mom, I'll call her original pediatrician who treated her after she was first born. Maybe he can run some more tests and see if there are any changes."

That very day, the pediatrician, Dr. Leverson, returned Marissa's call and told her to bring Willow in to see him. They went from there to the hospital. That was going to be the beginning of Willow's fight for survival. Many tests would be run and finally an exploratory operation was scheduled. Willow's kidney showed some kind of abnormality. Marissa and her mother, with her stepfather accompanying her, went to the children's hospital in the large city where they lived and waited for the operation to be over. One hour...two hours...three hours...and Marissa paced the floor...four hours...and finally in the fifth hour, the nurse and doctor came to say that she was out of surgery and into recovery and they would be able to see her shortly. Yes, she would be okay. There was a problem with one of the kidneys and the bladder, something about renal duplication, but they had fixed it with the operation and she should be fine.

Marissa hurried to the room to be by her child's side; there she lay on her left side with a large bandage covering her entire right side. It started at the right of her backbone and wrapped across and beneath her navel as if she had been almost guillotined in half. There were tubes leading from the bandage and bags hanging from the bed filling with fluids. Her child was groggily calling to her.

"Mommy, I'm thirsty, can I have a drink?"

"Willow, honey, not just yet, sweetheart, let Mommy get you a wet washcloth for your lips and tongue," Marissa whispered in the dark silent room.

Over and over through the long night would come the begging voice of the child crying for water, which Marissa had been forbidden to give her.

The danger was not over yet and the body needed to heal before too much liquid or food could be given, only the relentless drip, drip, drip to the IV in Willow's arm which was giving her painkilling medicines and drugs but was also drying her mouth unmercifully.

Then with the slow lightening of the skies outside the window and the hours of waiting finished, Marissa was instructed that now she could give the occasional ice chip.

So with her mother's constant attention, day by day Willow continued to improve, but first there was the solid food hurtle to get through and then the waiting for her bowels to move and mother and child both rejoiced when they finally did. Then the bandages began to get smaller and smaller and then one drain was removed and finally the final drain was taken out and the wait to see if Willow would pass water on her own. Of course she did, which sent Marissa into such a spasm of weeping for joy that the nurse came running to see if something bad had happened.

She was fine, so fine in fact that her mother was at her wit's end how to keep the child still and quiet. The doctors had advised that she not be too active. She healed quickly and came home four weeks later with the long scar which had almost sliced her in half. It would be a thorn in the side with the child when she became a teenager, but she would always be reminded "would you rather have been dead now" or with a scar.

Life again settled into a routine, with mother, grandmother, grandfather, and granddaughter, pulling together to maintain a healthy balance. There were very few bumps in the road, very few unusual happenings, until a fateful Christmas Eve.

It was like most Christmases, hectic and busy, and the usual round of office parties were in full swing. Marissa very seldom went to office parties anymore. After Willow's bout with the surgery, she stayed pretty close to home and hovered probably a little more than she should have. Willow was doing fine though and thoroughly enjoying have the undivided attention of her grandparents. So when Marissa called home to see how she was doing and mentioned having been invited to a Christmas party after work at a local pub, her mother suggested, "Go, don't stay too late, but have a little fun."

There was music playing and loud laughter in every corner of the room and not one chair available at any table, there were so many people there. Finally, Marissa climbed on a stool at the bar and ordered herself a drink. She looked around and didn't see the friend who had invited her, but saw that a man standing next to her was casting interested looks her way. She recognized him, of course, he was the senior manager in her department and everyone knew he was very married. So there was no danger here, she would never get involved with a married man.

They began to talk and then he turned to leave, but as he did, he brushed against her arm, and a lightning jolt of feeling jumped between them. How is it possible that that sudden jolt of feeling, that same electric shock of feeling that she had not felt since Stephen all those years ago, should happen here, in this bar, with this man? She could feel the tingling still vibrating in her arm.

Marissa was bewildered and confused. He looked back intently at her, and then was gone. Home to his wife, home to his upper class neighborhood, home to happiness and children and she wished that she was in that home at that moment in time. What was the matter with her? The party was over for her and she hurried to leave and go home to her child, her parents, and her troubled existence. Would she ever have a life like that, with a man who hurried home to her?

She would not meet him again for some time. He would be transferred to another branch of the company, and though she would look for him at work, she looked in vain. He was not there.

Jeffery Delclare left the bar, looking over his shoulder at the young woman he had left sitting on the stool. He knew he had to get out of there right now, there was something about her that tugged at him. What was it that he felt, stirring in his mind? He loved his wife, there was no doubt in his mind about that. But the attraction to the young woman had been elemental and lightning fast and he knew that he had better get out of there before he said or did something he would be sorry for. Well, the Christmas holidays were long at the publishing company and it would be more than a week before he would return to work. He would have a grip on himself before he went back, that was for sure. And as for her, he was sure he hadn't given any overt signals or would need to make any apologies. She probably hadn't noticed the spark that he had felt at all. He would put it behind him, the upper management team had requested a meeting with him on returning after the holidays, he would think about that. And so he finished the drive home and entered to find the family waiting to go to midnight services at their church.

The day after New Year's Day was typically a slow day at most businesses and the same was true at the publishing company. If it weren't for the meeting with the bosses, he probably would have taken another day of vacation to recover from the seemingly endless rounds of parties, visits, and holiday celebrations that had engulfed them this year. Why did Christmas always seem so frantic? What had happened to the days of just visiting the old folks and staying at home with the kids and their toys? Well, there was no help for it, he would go in and see what he could do for them, if anything.

He pulled into the parking lot of the company and, there she was, the woman from the bar on Christmas Eve. She was just entering the building; he would wait until she was safely in before leaving his car. No use bumping into her in the parking lot. That would be awkward. The meeting was in 15 minutes. He would go straight to the boss's office and wait there until time to start. Then he would decide what if anything to do about bumping into her and what he would say, if anything. Did he want to say anything? Of course, he did, but would he? No, unless it was to return a "hello" in the hall or a nod and a smile. That was as far as it could go.

He reached the outer office of his boss's suite and told the secretary seated outside why he was there.

"Of course, Mr. Delclare, go right on in, they are waiting for you," she replied.

He entered the office and saw the president and vice president of the division, which he worked for, already there and waiting for him. Didn't these guys ever go home?

"Good morning, sir," Jeff said.

"Good morning, Jeff." The president indicated a chair and motioned for him to sit.

"You wanted to see me?"

"Yes, Jeff, Tom and I wanted to talk to you about a proposition we have for you."

"A proposition?" Jeff countered.

"Yes, we think that you are just the man we need to head up the operations out on the West Coast, in Oregon. In fact, we are wondering whether you and your family would be willing to relocate for a few years to help us get the operations out there up to snuff."

"Would this be a permanent move or would we be coming back, and what about our home here?" Jeff wondered.

"We would buy your home here and purchase one out there for you for your stay. I think you would like the area, it is not far from the ocean and you once said that you liked to fish. After the division is up to speed, we believe that a position here at the main office at your new level may become available. We can talk further on this, though, after you have given your new job some experience."

"Well, the children are still small, so I guess they could survive the move, I wouldn't like to do it when they are in high school. I think it might be too hard on them then to give up their friends and hobbies. Do I have to give you a decision right now, can I talk with my wife and call you?"

"Of course, but it does carry a VP title and a generous increase in salary, too? Think about it, talk to her and give us a call. If you decide you want the job, you better start packing and don't bother to come back here, just let us know and the moving vans can be at your place as soon as you are ready to leave."

"I'll call you in the morning," Jeff said.

"Go on home and talk it over the rest of today with the whole family."

He left the office after advising his secretary about his potential shift in area and gave her directions on what to do with his personal belongings. As he was leaving the building, the young woman who had captured his eye turned down a hallway to the copy room and was gone. It was just as well that he leave the main office, there were going to be problems if he stayed here.

March 1843

It was cooler on deck than in the cabin. She had been ill for the last two days but she was feeling better now and a walk on deck in the cool evening was better than being cooped up in the tiny cabin any longer. Two days out of London on this ship and the weather had turned unpleasant with rolling swells that tossed the ship up and down along with her stomach. The winds had calmed and now the ship rode smoothly and she felt that she was at last getting her sea legs. There were a few other hardy souls wandering in among the sailors who were busy trimming the sails and repairing the canvas. There in front of her was a couple in their early thirties, she thought. As they turned to walk in the opposite direction, she nodded hello to them. The woman smiled and walked forward to her with her hand outstretched.

"Good evening, Miss, or is it, Mrs. Barrett?" she asked.

"Good evening, you have me at a disadvantage, madam, for I do not know your name while you are familiar with mine," answered Cathy.

The woman laughed. "Of course, I do, I am the wife of Captain Smith and I get to read all the passengers' names off of the register. I am so glad to have the company of a young woman on this voyage. I am traveling back to the United States after a visit with my parents in England."

"Well then, it is Miss, Mrs. Smith. I, too, am happy to have female companionship on this voyage."

"If you are now feeling well enough, the captain and I would like you to join our table for dinner tomorrow."

"Yes, to be sure, we would welcome your company for every evening, if it is to your liking," the captain confirmed.

"That is very gracious and I would welcome the conversation with you both. This is the first time I have been to the United States and am most curious as to what I will find on my arrival in New York."

"Well, then we shall have much to talk about as we live in New York ourselves when my husband is in port."

"Thank you for your kind offer and I will dine with you tomorrow evening," Cathy replied and then continued on her walk in need of exercise and fresh air.

The next evening she was shown into the captain's cabin and beheld a table set with silver and crystal and the food prepared and steaming for their appetites. After the dinner was begun and the claret had been poured, they settled back to talk about the New World. The captain's wife was ebullient in her praise of the place and went to great lengths to extol the beauty of the land and the opportunity for a person to rise above their station and become wealthy and even famous. There was a great deal of commerce and comings and goings and the arts were favored as well, with theaters and musicales and every sort of entertainment that one would wish. There were publishers and magazines and newspapers and writers of every sort. Yes, indeed, the United States had much to offer someone willing to work.

Catherine listened with a careful ear to all she was told. Truly this was a wonderful place, but, of course, until she had safely landed and seen for herself she would take the flowery descriptions with a grain of salt. Her mamma had always said the grass always looked greener on the other side of the fence, but that is because you didn't look straight down at the cow manure that made it that way. She would reserve judgment until she had seen for herself.

So the days continued one after another and Catherine found herself being welcomed by the captain's wife as a friend and confidante. She was given secrets and hopes to share in with the young woman and they grew closer still. Catherine could not bring herself to divulge the truth about herself and said only that she had nothing to hold her in the old country and had decided on gaining an inheritance to strike out for new horizons after her mamma had died. That at least was true, though she continued to think of Daniel and his smoldering eyes.

She did invite her new friend to read some of the poetry that she had been writing as the ship moved ever closer to the country she was traveling to. Caroline Smith was taken with the depth of feeling and serious thought displayed by the verses.

"Catherine, you must try and publish your work in New York. You have a great gift; you shouldn't hide it. God gives each of us different gifts and yours is obviously in the written word. Continue to write and find someone to publish your work. There are several good magazines which I am sure would welcome your submissions."

"Do you really think that they are worth sending. It is just something I have always liked to do and found extremely satisfying. I never thought of publishing. Maybe you are right, after I am settled and have time I will explore the possibility. While we are on the subject of settling, can you recommend a good area to purchase property there? I need to find a place to live and I am told that there will be enough funds available for me to own property."

"My dear," Caroline whispered, "you will have to find a barrister to handle all the legal affairs since you are a single woman. But if I had all the money I wanted with which to buy land, I would buy on Long Island. That is the fairest part of New York, just a short ferry ride to the mainland, but always blessed with sea breezes even in the summer when New York can be stifling. Yes, by all means, buy on Long Island and I shall visit you all the time," she finished laughing heartily.

"Hmm, I have always liked the seashore, perhaps that is a good plan. I have a letter of introduction to a barrister there in New York, maybe he will be able to help me."

"Until your house is built, you will, of course, stay with me. I wouldn't have it any other way. No arguments now, Captain Smith is often out to sea and I am lonely. I have prayed for children but so far God has not seen fit to bless me. Perhaps one day, but you most certainly must stay with us."

"You are so kind to me, if you insist and put it so, how can I refuse? And when the house is built you will be my guest at every opportunity," Catherine agreed.

And so the two spent the days planning the building of the new house and the fun they would have finding furnishings and such, and slowly but surely the days were accomplished for her arrival in New York.

It was early one morning and the seagulls were spinning overhead, when the sailor high aloft called the long-awaited "Land ho." Catherine rushed on deck to look in all directions to see if she could sight it, too. Yes, far off on the horizon was a dark smudge, which gradually grew larger and larger. She had a paper in her hand and quickly folded it to give to her new friend.

"Caroline," Catherine said, "I have written something for you to celebrate our friendship and the kindness I have enjoyed from you. I hope you like it."

Caroline took the piece of paper that Catherine handed to her and opened it to read:

I Will Not Cry

If things go wrong and I am sad,
If plans won't work and times are bad
If friends turn their backs my way
If loved ones balk and ruin my day,
I will not cry.

If Dame Misfortune plagues my track,
If Fate steps in and holds me back
If my money's short and days are long
If my lips are silent, I'm without song
I will not cry.

And you may well ask me why
These things do not make me cry
I'll explain that all will end
That tears flow for, my friend.

But take from my life my dreams
And the showers from heaven, it seems
Will be as naught when likened to
The tears I'll shed for loss of you.

"Oh Catherine, you are so special and this is so special to me. Thank you for those wonderful thoughts!" Caroline exclaimed.

"You are very welcome, Caroline, and thank you so much for your wonderful friendship." And they turned to watch the horizon of the New York skyline grow ever larger and larger.

June 14, 1970

The phone rang. "Marissa, it's for you," her mother said.

"Hello," Marissa answered, "who is it?"

"Hi, Marissa, it's Stacey from work. We are running short of help here and I know it is your day off, but could you possibly get away and come and help us? We have this deadline and the vice president just came on line today and we really could use you if you can get here."

"Okay, okay, hold your horses." Marissa grumbled, "This had better be an emergency. My daughter's going to be really unhappy when she learns that I have to miss her campout again."

"It is an emergency and you can always go camping, so get your fanny in here and pull our bacon out of the fire with your flying fingers."

"All right, flattery will get you everything, I'll be there in 20 minutes,"

Marissa said, as she ran for the bathroom to put on her makeup and get her clothes in order.

"Mom, I'm sorry, they need me right now at work. Will you explain to Willow why I can't go camping with you all? Have a great time, you three, will you? Love to you all!" Marissa shouted as she ran down to her car.

All the way to work, she wondered what was the big rush that couldn't wait until Monday morning when she would have been back at work anyway. Oh well, the overtime would help out now that she no longer received any child support from the ne'er do well that she had been married to. He had decided to give up parental rights in lieu of having to pay child support, the jerk. Willow was just as well off without him, but she bet she would never be able to convince her of that. Little girls always wanted their daddies. She remembered wondering why she never saw hers very much when she was growing up. Then she didn't care anymore so it didn't matter. Or at least she told herself she didn't care and it was pretty much the same thing, wasn't it?

As she pulled into the parking lot at work, she noticed quite a few cars in the lot. Well, there must really be a rush after all. Must be a new author who is pushing for a certain deadline date. Let's see what all the excitement is about.

Marissa opened the door and rushed around the corner almost colliding with, of all people, the man at the bar on that Christmas Eve. What in the world was he doing here? Stacey hurried over to introduce the new vice president just transferred in from Seattle.

"Have you met Mr. Delclare, Marissa? He is our new vice president just transferred in from Seattle."

"Actually yes, we have met, but I don't think that Mr. Delclare would remember. Mr. Delclare, Marissa Feinstein." Marissa held out her hand to shake his. There it was again, that ripple up her arm, raising all the hairs on the back of her hand. Lightning!

"My pleasure, Miss, or is it Mrs. Feinstein? And you are wrong, I remember very well," he said as he kept hold of her hand.

"Oh, it's Ms., Mr. Delclare, Marissa's divorced," Stacey blurted out. Marissa gave her a stare and extricated her hand from his. Stacey had the grace to look chastised.

"It's Ms. Feinstein, Mr. Delclare, I am divorced and I have a four-year-old daughter who is very upset with me for missing our weekend camping adventure with her nana and papa, so I hope this rush really is a rush. I hate disappointing my daughter," replied Marissa.

66

"Yes, I'm sure you are in the doghouse now, and I am sorry about that but this is important."

Marissa threw herself into the project. She was a good typist and had always seemed to be able to pull the fat out of the fire, so by the end of the day it looked as though they might indeed meet the deadline. Perhaps after the weekend was over they would be able to wind it up.

She was leaving the building that evening, tired and sore, and wanting nothing more than a hot tub and a long soak. She noticed Mr. Delclare walking to his car and watched as he drove away. Why was she so attracted to him? What was there about him that drew her? He was taller than Stephen was and not so dark, but there were those same warm eyes that stole over her and the smile was special, too. Yes, he was definitely interesting. But out of reach with his slender gold band circling the third finger of his left hand. Definitely out of reach.

Several weeks had passed and it was during one of the lunch breaks when she had left the building to go out and catch a breath of the fine spring air, that she was to speak to him again. He had followed her from the building and watched as she strolled down the parking lot toward her car. She had a long confident stride, head up and watching in all directions for other cars or people to cross her path. She was beautiful, slender and young. What was he thinking of, he was probably too old for her? She deserved someone younger than he was. He had checked her personnel file quietly after he had returned. He was 10 years her senior. But then he remembered the look in her eyes that Christmas Eve. Maybe, just maybe, she felt the connection, too. He watched as she turned and started back to the building. As she came up the walk, he walked to her and stopped.

"Marissa, I have been wanting to talk to you."

"Yes sir, what can I do for you?"

"Well, I was thinking that maybe you might find it enjoyable, I mean you and your daughter might find it enjoyable, to join my family and I to see the Lippensteiner Stallions at the Auditorium next week."

"But isn't your wife attending?" Marissa murmured. "I wouldn't want to intrude."

"She can see from where she is very well without attending. She died a year and a half ago in an automobile accident, and I am sure her seat in heaven will be much better than ours."

"Oh, I'm so sorry, I didn't mean, I mean, I, well, thank you for the kind invitation and I am sure my daughter will enjoy seeing the horses, she is a fan of any kind of horse."

"Well that is good because my daughters don't do anything but eat, sleep, and talk those horses of ours."

"Oh, you own horses? I didn't realize that, but, of course, you would if they were really that crazy about them. I grew up with horses in the back yard, literally, and spent all the time I could across the fence petting them and playing with them. But my family didn't own them, they belonged to the wealthy neighbors across the fence."

"Perhaps you might come and ride with us some evening. We have extra mounts at the farm," Delclare asked.

"Perhaps," Marissa said.

CHAPTER SIX

April 1970

In less than one month, he would tie the knot. Cynthia was a young widow he had met on moving to South Carolina. They had begun by speaking to each other at the corner grocery where she was working as a checker, and over the past year, their romance had blossomed into a commitment to each other. Stephen hadn't known if he really wanted a commitment after Marissa. He didn't think that he would ever trust a woman again, but finally loneliness had sent him in search of female companionship, and he knew that he could trust Cynthia with his love.

He still had lingering thoughts of Marissa, but she was far away and married to another, he would get on with his life. He wasn't getting any younger and he wanted sons and daughters of his own. Cynthia had a passle of children, he hoped for one of his own to bond to. He loved her kids, but he wouldn't be complete without his own child. He hoped that Marissa was happy, he didn't wish her any ill will. He would probably always love her, in some small corner of his heart and mind. This fact would not interfere with his life with Cynthia, they would be happy, he would devote his life to making her happy again. To be widowed young with four children is not an easy thing. He would do his best to make her smile. And his job with the sheriff's office would keep him from being under foot too much. She was used to handling the kids. They would all be happy.

August 1970

It was several weeks later when her phone rang on her desk. On the other end was the voice of Jeffery Delclare.

"Marissa, can you get someone to take care of Willow this evening?"

"I suppose so, what is the problem?" Marissa thought he was probably going to ask her to work overtime again.

"No problem, but I was thinking of going to the farm tonight to check on the stock and wondered if you might like to come along and maybe take a ride. It is supposed to be an especially nice evening."

"Yes, I would enjoy it. How shall I dress? I don't have any boots."

"I think one of my daughters has a pair that will fit you, I'll bring them along. Just wear long trousers or jeans. You don't want to get saddle sores."

"Okay, what time shall I expect you to pick me up?"

"How about around 6:00 p.m. and we will grab a sandwich to take with us," Jeff stated.

"Sounds good, I'll see you at 6:00 p.m." Marissa hung up. Was this a date? Would his children be there, too? She didn't know but she was as excited as a schoolgirl. She had wondered if he had felt the connection, and the fact that he had remembered the night they had met at Christmas seemed to confirm that he had. Had her prayers been heard? Had she been alone long enough for God to take pity on her? She longed for a person to connect to that would fulfill her dreams and thoughts. She needed to be loved by someone who was completely committed to her. Could she trust Jeffery Delclare with her heart? She was ready to try again and to live, was he ready to put his memories behind him of his wife and see in her another chance? She was as anxious and excited as a high school girl.

6:00 p.m. There was his car pulling into the driveway. He parked the car and had almost reached the door when she opened it ready to dash out. He stopped her with a wave of his hand and came inside to speak with her parents. He was some years older than she was and he and her stepfather had much in common. He spent the better part of an hour talking and getting acquainted with her parents before he seemed to realize that the daylight was slipping away. He took her hand and they left the house to return to the car. He seemed to like holding her hand; she remembered how long he had kept it before when they had been introduced.

He opened the car door for her and after climbing in beside her, started down the lane. All the way to the farm, they talked of office things and the different cities where he had lived and worked in; and then about her life and what it had been like for her as a child. He was so easy to talk to. The car pulled up into a gravel road and wound up a hill to a large barn with a hayloft above. She jumped from the car to walk into the barn and heard the horses softly nickering and munching on their hay. Jeffrey came behind her to introduce her to the animals. They all had names. He was riding a mount called Cinnamon Cloud and he showed her one called Princess who was quite tame and old, but for her first try in a long time it seemed a good choice. He motioned for her to continue to acquaint herself with the animals while he finished his inspection of a water pipe problem that had been brought to his attention. After that inspection was finished, he pulled some boots from the trunk of the car and handed them to Marissa.

"Here, try these on and see if they fit. They belong to my oldest girl, Leslie. My other girl, Sandy, has really small feet like mine so I knew better than to bring hers."

Marissa pulled off her shoes and tugged at the boots. They were a little small but if she didn't have to walk too far they would do.

"What about your boy, does he ride too?"

"No, Leon is more of a mechanical type, if you know what I mean."

"Oh, you mean he wants to feed it gas instead of grass." She laughed.

"Yes, that's exactly what I mean. Well, let's saddle a couple of horses and go for a ride," he said.

The night was magnificent, with the sun just setting and the dusk beginning to descend. And every now and then a star twinkled in the darkening sky.

The horses saddled, they both mounted their animals. Marissa was nervous, it had been years since she had been on a horse. She hoped she didn't fall off. But it seemed to be like riding a bicycle, once you learned you never forgot. She felt marvelous, light and free and inhibited. What was wrong with her? She never felt this free. He had the most invigorating effect on her, like champagne let out of the bottle, which bubbled and bubbled in the glass. That was how she felt. She felt like champagne.

Jeffery watched the metamorphous unfold as she sat her horse and carefully inclined her head to encourage the old mare to go forward. She looked like a child discovering chocolate for the first time. It was enlightening to see the professional typist and mother turn into a child in front of his eyes. He wanted to prolong that moment forever. Would it be possible to capture this child and keep her? He was going to try.

With that invitation was to begin a lifetime of sharing. Mr. Delclare became Marissa's answer to prayer. There were dinners and theater outings, picnics and neighborhood potlucks, dancing to music at company parties. There were evenings at home after his children were in bed, with a fire in the fireplace and a bottle of wine in the cooler, when they would share all the painful memories in their lives. Mr. Delclare became Jeffery, and then Jeff and Marissa became Missy and the lightning flashed between them and held them in thrall.

The tempest of emotion and feeling that had lay dormant for the past three years burst into flame and they became swept away.

Jeff would always call Missy before her eyes closed in sleep at her home, even though they had spent the entire evening together. When he would be traveling for the company, the last voice Missy would hear each night would be his. All the unhappiness and disappointments of the past were being swept away by his unending caring and complete devotion and the days and nights melted slowly into one.

Missy was to find herself pondering on her feelings, and one evening as she was waiting for him to pick her up, her happiness welled up inside her and she picked up her pencil and pad and began to write. The poetry flowed from her like a river and line after line spilled onto the page. All her hopes for the future and love for him came tumbling out. Should she give it to him? Should she let him really know what was simmering in her heart and soul? Could she trust him to be gentle with her thoughts that she was committing to paper?

They were sitting at dinner, enjoying looking into each other's eyes reveling in the wonder at having been in the right place at the right time for each of them. Missy reached into her purse and pulled forth a folded piece of paper. She looked at him deeply and sighed.

"What's the big sigh for?" Jeff asked.

"I have something for you, but I am afraid you won't like it or will laugh."

"What is it?" he said.

"Just a poem I have for you to read."

"Well, what are you waiting for, let me read it."

"Okay, but you have to promise not to laugh." She smiled.

Missy handed him the paper and watched as he unfolded it and began to read. He looked at her with a warm smile on his face.

"This is great, it sounds just like us. Where did you find it?"

"I didn't find it," she replied, "I wrote it."

"You wrote it! It is great, it is wonderful, and it says all the things I am thinking but haven't been able to put into words. You have reached into my heart and pulled out my feelings here."

"I am so glad you like it," she said, "it just came to me as I was sitting waiting for you to pick me up."

"You mean, you wrote this while waiting for me to pick you up this evening?"

"Yes."

"Missy, I love you, you are wonderful." Jeff grinned. "How many men can say they have been courted by a poet?"

"I love you too, so very much, my darling."

He looked at her with such love in his eyes, she felt her heart soaring higher and higher, and then he took her hands and spoke, "Marissa, can you get your mother to watch Willow for you for a few days?" Jeff questioned, looking long and hard into her eyes.

"Why, I suppose so, why do you ask?" Marissa wondered as she felt him squeeze her hands and then draw her to him.

"We have been together with the children so much, we really haven't had a time to ourselves. We need to get away and be together for a while. I have a conference coming up in the Seattle office with some of the management there and I thought you would enjoy coming along and getting away from New York for a while. What do you say, are you game?"

"But we aren't married, what would people say? I would like to go with you but I don't want the children to suffer."

"Don't worry, Miss Prude," he laughed, "we will have separate rooms. But people will talk anyway so you just have to take a chance. What do you say?"

"I say, yes, my dear." Marissa smiled and hugged him even tighter. But in her heart she wondered if she was making a mistake. The temptations away from the children might be too great. Was she a prude? After all, it was the seventies. She had better think about her actions before she leaped. She remembered a fateful night in the fifties when she had leaped and thought she had it all, but then she had thrown it away. She didn't want to jeopardize her relationship with Jeffery, she loved him too much. But Seattle sounded heavenly and she could surely keep her emotions in check for a weekend. After all, she was almost thirty now, it wasn't like she was a silly teenager.

May 1843

It was stuffy in the office although all the windows were thrown open in an attempt to catch an early morning breeze. The buildings that were crowded so close together in this city of thousands kept any hope of a breeze away. Cathy had been waiting for almost twenty minutes in the outer offices of Masseurs Thompson, Crawford, and Harriman, Attorneys at Law, New York

City, New York. She clutched the letters of introduction, which she had carried from England. She knew she should have sent word ahead that she was coming but didn't want to wait for the reply, she needed the funds. Her friends, Caroline and the captain, had welcomed her into their home most graciously, but she didn't want to impose on them unnecessarily.

The door to the inner offices slowly opened and an older man slightly built stepped toward her and beckoned to her to come forward. She rose from the chair she was sitting on and walked toward the door.

"Miss Barrett, I am sorry you have had to wait so long, if I had known you were coming I would have cleared my calendar, please come in, come in." He motioned for her to take a seat opposite him and sat down to appraise her. "My name is Peter Crawford, Attorney, at your service."

Catherine seated herself and thrust the letters she had been clutching toward him. "I should have sent word ahead of me, it is I who am sorry for the inconvenience, but I was in a hurry to start my new life here in this country and I knew I needed to speak with an attorney to do that. These letters will properly introduce me and I hope you are in a position to set up accounts for me and obtain property in my name so that I may start on a residence here."

"To be sure, I can do all those things," he said, as he opened the letters and began to read. "Hmm, yes, I know this bank, it is the same as I keep my accounts in and I know the banker well, there should be no problem in getting these funds released to your use. Had you any idea what kind of home you plan on building or where you would like to live? I have several properties myself which are available for sale if you would be interested."

"I'm not sure yet what type of home I need, but when I find the property perhaps some architect here can advise me on what kind of house would complement the site," Catherine proposed. "I am presently a guest of Captain Smith's, and his wife and I have become great friends. She suggested that a property on Long Island might be something I would like."

"Yes, I am sure that area would suit you, perhaps a little isolated but certainly one of the most beautiful in the surrounding area. I think I might own a piece that you may find pleasing. Let me see to the opening of the accounts and getting your funds at your disposal and we can make an appointment to visit the property I own there and see what you think," Mr. Crawford said.

"Please advise me when this is accomplished and we will go whenever you have the time. My time is completely free now and I can go whenever I please."

So with the promise to notify her as soon as possible in the matter of her accounts, Mr. Crawford put Catherine in her coach and bade her goodbye.

Before the week was out, she received a communiqué that Mr. Crawford would be pleased to accompany Miss Catherine Barrett, and any of her acquaintances she might wish to invite, to visit the property under perusal on Friday next. Catherine gave the messenger her affirmative reply and when Friday came she and Caroline along with Captain Smith were waiting for Mr. Crawford to arrive.

The four of them climbed into his carriage and made for the harbor. After waiting there for 20 minutes in a salon, a ferry pulled in to take them to Long Island. Mr. Crawford had arranged for suitable conveyance to be available once they arrived and they were boarded in an open carriage and driven out along the seashore. The vistas were gorgeous and the day sunny and bright. Catherine looked first one way and then the other and the beauty outshone anything she had seen thus far. Then the road took a turn to the left and they began to climb to the top of a large hill. From this vantage point, she was able to see the ferry dock and across the harbor the outline of buildings in New York. She imagined that at night the lights from the streets of the city would be visible even here. She looked at Mr. Crawford.

"Are there water and heating supplies here, and how will I be provided with foodstuffs isolated here? How often does the ferry run and would servants be available to work for her here in the house?"

All good questions, Mr. Crawford thought, here was no foolish woman taken in by the beauty only, she was practical, too.

"There is much agriculture here, Miss Barrett, and also the ocean provides plenteous bounty with local fisherman selling their catches in the markets hereabouts daily. And the island is well watered with springs, ponds and lakes abounding. I am sure when you begin to build you will have no trouble finding servants eager and willing to work for you."

"What is the name of this place that we are standing on now?" she asked.

"The natives call it 'Seacliff,'" he replied.

"What price are you asking for the land, how much land is included in the sale, and are there mineral rights as well?" she said.

"There are a hundred acres in this piece that I own. That land that runs to the edge of the cliff and then below to the sea, and then is bounded on one side by the stream which runs in all weather and on the other side by a gorse hedge, which I will have flagged for you. The price for this land on today's market is $5.00 an acre or $500.00," he answered.

"Do I have that much in my estate?"

"Oh yes, you have that much and more, never fear you will be able to build a grand house here." He laughed.

"I don't know about a grand house, I will be satisfied with a house that allows me to view the countryside from all directions and opens to the breezes. I am wanting to build a home." She sighed. "I will take it and you can draw up the papers for me to sign. Also if you can oblige me in the matter of an architect that would also be a great help," Catherine said.

"To be sure, I think I have a man in mind who might suit you well. I will send him around. His name is Matthew Davis."

Many meetings and hours later the house began to take shape on paper and Catherine watched as the architect faithfully paid attention to all her ideas. The house would be two storied with porches and verandahs on the lower level and balconies at the windows and doors on the upper floor. The building material would be stone in a soft brown patina and when the sunset's light would touch it the whole building would have a golden glow. She could visualize it in her mind. Somewhere she could write and wander along the cliffside and think about her life and Daniel faraway on the other shore.

Meanwhile on that faraway shore, someone was looking westward and chaffing at delays. Daniel had interrogated his coachman after he had received the letter and poem from Catherine. The timbre of the poem troubled him, there was irony and cynicism in every line, and pain, that he could almost reach out and feel the pain dropping from every word. Why hadn't he gone with her? It turned out that the business he had had to conduct had not come to a good return and he would have been better off going with her and canceling his appointments for the week. Drat, he knew that she had gone to see a barrister. But now his mother had become ill, too ill to leave and he was forced once again to bide his time before going to London and picking up the trail. He hoped that Cathy would not forget him with all this delay or think that he had forgotten her. Poor mother, she had not planned to become ill. But when does anyone ever plan to become ill. There was no help for it though he must stay in England until he was sure she would recover. He could not leave now. He would go as soon as his mother was better!

Meanwhile on Long Island, the house contract was let and construction began to make it take the shape shown on the papers the architect had drawn.

She and Caroline spent many hours pouring over samples of carpet and draperies and wall coverings and paint. It was becoming a monumental task and she needed a break. Caroline suggested that it was time that they did some socializing and arranged for her to be introduced to the company of writers who gathered at one patron's home on Friday evenings.

Captain Smith, along with Caroline and Catherine, entered the doors of the salon of Frederika Bremer. They waited for their host to acknowledge them. She was chatting with a group of people, when she turned her head and noticed them. Quickly excusing herself, she hurried to their sides.

"Forgive me, I forget my hostess duties, please come and be welcome. I was just talking with some of my contemporaries and got caught up in a debate." She laughed sweetly. "You are Captain Smith and the lovely Caroline, but who is this sweet child?"

Caroline pulled Catherine forward to introduce her. "This is my dear friend, Catherine Aurora Barrett, late of England, come to settle here with us."

"Catherine Barrett, you are welcome, we were just getting ready to take our seats for a reading by one of my great friends and helpful publisher, Edgar Allan Poe. Please make yourselves comfortable while I seat my other guests."

The woman floated away from them and motioned with her hands for attention. "Please, everyone, take your seats. Please, Mr. Poe has another one of his deliciously evil stories to read for us tonight."

There was a podium in the center of the room and a small raised platform, and upon it stood a very handsome man. He was slight of build, with dark black hair and sunken eyes, which burned with intensity, and he held his manuscript tightly in his left hand. He didn't seem steady on his feet but then the port and claret had been freely given the entire preface to this time, so it was understood that he had had his share. Though it was all forgotten when he opened his mouth to speak.

The words echoed and eerily vibrated from his lips and the story of the "Murders of the Rue Morgue" unfolded in the listener's minds. What a gory tale, but told with such description that one could imagine being in the places and seeing the awful things in their entirety. What genius had the man to be able to think and describe these things? Catherine was held enthralled. She would never be the writer that this person was. Never in a million years would she be able to stir someone so. Even so the story unraveled to its conclusion and Poe took his accolades in stride and then thanking his hostess for her kindness took his leave.

Caroline was disappointed that he left without lingering. This was the very man she had wanted Catherine to meet. Well, they would just have to try again. There would be other salons she was sure. Yes, they would come again, but perhaps it would be best to wait until the house was finished. She knew that Catherine had not written a word since the start of the project; after it was completed, then there was time.

September, 1970

Seattle was wonderful. Most days Jeffery was in meetings, but in the evenings they would dine at the Needle or wander the streets looking at shops, musing to each other about the wonder of finding each other. They did have separate rooms, but the last night of their trip, Marissa heard a knock at her door. She had finished her toiletries and almost turned the bed down when it came. A gentle tapping at the door. She crossed to the door and peered out into the hall from the peephole. There in the hallway staring back at her stood Jeffery, with the largest bouquet of red roses she had ever seen. She threw on a gossamer thin robe over her pj's and opened the door just a crack.

"Jeff, what are you doing here now? We just said goodnight," Marissa said opening the door a little wider.

"I know, but I saw an all-night florist shop and couldn't resist bringing these to you." He noticed the tan lines under the robe and felt his resolve slipping. He had only meant to bring the flowers, nothing more, but now the closeness of her scent and the heady arousal of his own body propelled him into the room.

"Marissa, I will go if you really want me to, but you must tell me to go right now, otherwise I think I will never leave you again," Jeffery stated as he closed the door behind him and laying the flowers on the dresser, pulled her to him.

"I don't want you to go. I wish we could stay here forever," she murmured with her lips against his own and the feel of his strength against her.

"I love you, darling, don't worry that I will ever hurt you," he returned and picked her up to place her on the bed close by.

"I believe you, Jeffery, I know you won't hurt me. Just don't think badly of me tomorrow," she answered.

"I want all your tomorrows, so never fear that I will think badly of you then," Jeff said as he removed his clothes and settled himself beside her.

"Kiss me, Marissa, kiss me and never let me go." Jeff smiled.

August 1971

Months went by, months filled with delicious moments and sharing between Marissa and Jeffery, picnics in evenings with the two of them lying side by side watching the stars streaked across the summer skies. Evenings with the children vying for their attention and accolades at horse events in competitions. And after seeing each other almost every night and most of the days at work, one hot August evening, Jeff came to Missy's home to pick her up for dinner and a movie. Her roommate, Anna, was keeping Willow and her own daughter for the evening and had taken the girls for an ice cream. Jeff took Missy in his arms and handed her a small velvet box. Missy looked at Jeff and then at the box.

"Missy, will you do me the honor of becoming my wife. Will you marry me?" Jeff asked with hesitancy in his voice.

Missy looked into his eyes and saw in truth the complete devotion there. She knew this was not a mistake. This was perhaps what God had been preparing her for through all the unhappiness and mistakes of the past. She was not afraid of losing him or failing him. There were no ghosts of Stephen wandering in her mind. She was finally home.

"Yes, Jeff, I will. I love you more than life itself," Missy answered. "Thank you for loving me, too."

It was a moment to hold fast in her heart, one to bring out and remember when the troubled times ahead would threaten to overwhelm her. Although, now there was a wedding to plan and the task of breaking the news to the children, she was ready to begin her new life. Now Willow would have sisters and brothers, cousins, aunts and uncles. All the extended family that Mr. Delclare laid claim to. They decided to have a summer wedding the next year and involve as much of the family in the ceremony as possible. The children would all have a part so that they could feel as much a part of the marriage as their parents. A garden wedding was planned for the outdoors and Missy prayed for warm dry weather.

The day dawned bright and shining, a gorgeous day of summer sunshine and gentle breezes that caught at tendrils of soft golden brown hair and twisted them in the wind. The bride was radiant in blue; after all, white was for first weddings and virginity and all those first time things, but blue must have been lucky because the couple was blessed by happiness from the first.

All those ugly memories soon faded. Jeff was as loving a father to his new daughter as he was to his own. Missy found companionship not only with her new husband, but with his children as well. For fortune would separate them again and she would turn to her daughters for companionship and fun. The publishing business is a very competitive business and authors like to meet their publishers but are an eccentric group and like to be treated as divas and catered to. Many weeks, Jeff would be flying from city to city conferring with his clients, but never did a night go by when he was gone that the phone didn't ring for a goodnight call. She would hear the beloved voice whispering to her, "I love you, Missy, and I can't wait to get back home to you." And lying there upon the pillows, hearing the words that fed her soul, she whispered in return, "I love you, too, my darling. Hurry home to us all."

As the company prospered, he delegated those duties of travel and client pampering to his staff and was able to be with his family more.

"Missy," yelled Jeff, "where are my car keys? I am late for work and I lent them to you to take the cleaning into the drycleaners."

"Oh, Jeff, I don't know, you know how forgetful I am sometimes. Take my car and I will look for them and switch with you today."

"Missy, Missy, why can't you put them back when you have finished with them?" Jeff softened his tone and shook his head.

"I know I should, but with the kids, the horses, cows and all to take care of, I can hardly remember my own name or what day it is sometimes."

"Well, just call me and let me know if you find them," he called shaking his head as he headed out the door.

Missy didn't know what was happening to her, she just couldn't seem to get everything done since they had moved to the new house at the farm. It had seemed a good idea to rebuild so that the children could have the country air and the horses there for use whenever they felt like riding. Only there were many more chores now. It seemed like there was always something to be done. And lately she had gotten involved in a book club and that was just one more thing in her already busy life. But she really enjoyed the book club and Jeff had encouraged her to get more involved; after all, she was a writer. She should be involved with books and the ideas they inspired. After they had married, he had wanted her to be home with the children instead of working and she had agreed, so she had quit her job at the publishing company.

"After all," he had said, "someday the kids are going to be grown and gone. What if something happens to me? I am getting older all the time and I'm already 10 years older than you are? I could be gone too someday. You need friends of your own, people you like visiting and socializing with."

"You aren't going anywhere without me," she said. "I am going first, there is no longevity in my family anyway."

Jeff shook his head and looked lovingly at her, but he knew that someday she would be alone and he worried for her peace of mind when he was gone. She depended too heavily on his presence in her life for her stability. Perhaps having this book club outlet would be just the thing for her.

Missy had become very homebound since her marriage, not because she had to, but because now that she could be at home with her children, she coveted the time. For all the years that she struggled to keep herself afloat with Willow, now she could relax and enjoy their school years and the running of her home and farm. She was not a recluse by any stretch of the imagination, she was busy choring animals, horses, cows, and chickens, minding a large garden that filled the family larder, and mingling with her neighbors.

One such neighbor became her real friend in those days because of their common interest in their faith and family. Della lived across the hills to the east and Missy would jump into her car and drive the short distance to see her. One afternoon when she was motoring there, she rounded the bend in the drive to see a large brown Guernsey cow munching at the fence. This was a new addition to Della's menagerie and Missy hurried into the house to ask about it.

"Della," Missy cried, "where did you get the cow? What are you going to do with it? Are you really going to milk it? Would you teach me how?"

"Whoa," laughed Della, "one question at a time. Daddy and I are going to milk her and sure I'll teach you how."

Della's father spent summers with her and her husband Mike. He was a farmer and carpenter, and jack of all trades, could build anything, do anything, and knew just about everything. Missy loved talking with him; he was easy going and fun to be around.

"When can you teach me? I wish I had a cow like that, I have always wanted one. But Jeff says they tie you down too much and what would we do with all the milk. He has a million reasons why not to get one. But if you had one, maybe we could share it. You know, you milk once a day and I milk the other, and split the grain and hay costs and then split the milk. What do you think? It would work, I think."

Della looked at her trying to decide if she was really serious. It would be a help to have someone else able to milk in an emergency, what if her dad and she were both unable to milk one day!

"You talk it over with Jeff and I will discuss this with Dad and tomorrow we will all get together and talk it over," Della said.

Missy hurried home to garner her arguments to use in the upcoming discussion with Jeff. With four kids, the groceries were a drain on the budget but with all the milk, cream, and butter they wanted, they could even do ice cream and cheese and cottage cheese. She was really getting excited about this.

That evening as they were having dinner she broached the subject.

"Jeff, what would you say to the idea of splitting a milk cow with the neighbors?"

"Like in butchering for the freezer kind of splitting!"

"No, like in sharing expenses and the milking chores and the milk."

"How much expenses are we talking about here, and how much milk and what would I have to do in this whole plan?"

"The only thing you would have to do is buy some grain and give some of the hay we already raise. I would do all the milking and taking care of using the milk."

"How much milk are we talking about here?"

"Well, Della says that a Guernsey cow will give about 2 gallons of milk twice a day," Miss replied, "so our share would be about 14 gallons a week."

"What would you do with all that milk?"

"Well, I could make cheese and ice cream, and yogurt, and cottage cheese and surely I could find some needy family who would take the rest of it off my hands," Missy said in a rush.

"And where is this Guernsey cow coming from, who is going to buy her?"

"Oh that's easy, Della has already bought her."

"Oh, now I understand, Della has a cow and now you want a cow and you know that I won't be tied down to a cow, so you want me to let you co-own Della's cow. Well, if you want to do the milking and take care of the milk, it's up to you. You know I never could refuse you anything. Sounds like a plan to me."

And so the deal was struck on the following day, and Missy could hardly wait to go over early the next morning and get her first lesson in milking. She found that she was a natural at it and she and the cow got along famously. The cool mornings were always quiet and still when she would creep into the neighbor's barn and get the feed and hay ready for "Blossom's" breakfast and Blossom would be standing at the gate waiting to come in and stand in the stanchion. Della had a milking machine, but Missy preferred to do her milking by hand and would sit with her head against Blossom's warm stomach and draw the milk forth. She would be filled with a soft warm center, as though all the musings of the universe were congealing in her soul. Her thoughts would fly away from the dark barn and the soft swishing of the cow's mouth as Blossom rustled in the feedbox for the last few bits of grain and then reached over for the summer-scented hay to munch. Sometimes the rain would fall with a staccato sound on the tin-roofed barn and she would imagine herself in a war zone and under fire and see the lightning strikes as explosions of war machines filling the air with sound.

Her poetry began to flow again and many mornings she would rush home to put the milk away and grab her pad and pencil and start scribbling away while having her coffee. In the evenings, she would share those writings with Jeff as she sat after dinner with her wine and snuggled in his arms.

CHAPTER SEVEN

September 2001

The years were rushing by, first one and then another child climbed the stairs of the platform to have their hands shaken by the superintendent of schools and receive the rolled scrolls that would propel them into the world outside their parents' home. Now there were no Blossoms left in the barnyard, no children in the house, and there hardly seemed to be any inspiration left in her.

Leslie had married early, right after enrolling in her first year in college. She had decided that college was not for her and wanted her own husband and home. The couple followed the military to North Dakota and letters brought news of snow to the rooftops and talk of starting a family.

Sandy waited longer, but she too found a husband from her school years and married.

Leon couldn't wait to see the world and so immediately after finishing with his high school years, he signed to the Navy and was somewhere under the Pacific gliding along underwater protecting his country.

Finally, Willow also decided that marriage was for her and after a lovely ceremony in the family's Rock Church, left her parents' home to join herself in holy wedlock.

Marissa and Jeffery were empty nesters now and reveling in all the new freedom that it brought. But she was having trouble focusing on her writing. She now had all the time in the world but nothing to write about. The book club she had been a member of for these many years would have to spark any new inspirations, if there were going to be any.

She would have to finish reading the new selection in a hurry and check with the librarian on new selections in the morning before going to the club meeting.

Marissa was running late for her meeting and needed to drop off the book that she had finished to the library. Her friend at the check-in counter of the

that she try to publish in a weekly. I had hoped that Edgar Poe would be here tonight that I might introduce them. She has written some very eloquent poetry and I am sure that he would enjoy it."

"Of course he will be here, unless his wife is worse, which could be the case. She is in very poor health, and he fears for her. I don't know what will happen if he loses her, it is already affecting his mind, I think. He is supposed to read another of his works tonight, I hope it is a little happier than the others of late."

"How sad for him, to have found a love and then to have it threatened to be taken away. I don't know if I could survive losing someone I really loved. My mamma was that for me, but she was old and I knew I could not keep her forever. How sad to lose a soulmate at such a tender age. What is she, thirty-something?"

"Yes, I believe so, and they are so devoted to one another. Childhood sweethearts I'm told. Even cousins, I think!"

"Such a pity," Catherine said.

"You must excuse me now, I see some others I must greet, please take your refreshments and I will see you later." Fredrika hurried away to greet some late arrivals.

The three of them wandered to the table and tasted of the array of fruits and sweets that were offered and then began to circulate through the room. There were others there, which Caroline recognized and she was quick to introduce Catherine to them. The men were always interested in the introduction, while the women held back and watched the dark-haired beautiful young woman nod first to one and then to another.

She was slender and small, with long fingers that were unadorned by rings or other glaring jewelry. Her hands moved expressively when she talked and described things about her house that everyone had heard about. It and her presence were all the community of artists had talked about; and there were several landscape painters who wanted to be invited to her home to paint both she and it.

As she talked about her new residence, she became more and more animated and the gaslights of the room threw shimmering shadows in her eyes and hair. Caroline watched as she captivated her audience and had no doubts that were she to throw this kind of party, it would be well received.

Fredrika, meanwhile, was talking in a quiet way to a gentleman across the room who glanced across to where the young woman who was encircled with listeners stood. There was something about her, some familiarity that he wondered about. What was it that he could see there? Hmm, best to be introduced and see if conversation would shine some light on it.

Right now he had a duty to his hostess, his reading came next, afterwards he would catch the eye of Fredrika for an introduction. He stepped slowly to the podium as before and took from his coat pocket a scrap of paper. It was something he had scribbled in the night while watching at his wife's bedside. Not exactly in the same category as the "Murders of the Rue Morgue," but he thought it slightly entertaining. Fredrika was calling for attention and finally after seating themselves comfortably before him, all eyes turned his way.

Quietly, his voice began the story of "The Raven" and once again Catherine was mesmerized by the poetry. Here was another poet, not just a storyteller, but a real poet. Not of lighthearted verse but of poetry that spoke of tragedy and heartbreak and all those things of the darkness. She was breathless in anticipation of each line of the piece until at last he finished with the "nevermore." The company applauded, her among them, as he took his bows. Then when the uproar had ebbed, he glanced at Fredrika and she led him to Catherine.

"Catherine, I would like you to meet a very great artist and a very great friend of mine, Edgar Allan Poe," Fredrika said. "Edgar, may I present Miss Catherine Aurora Barrett." He blinked as he heard the name. Of course, he had thought her manner familiar, but perhaps the name was a coincidence. There were lots of Barretts in the world after all.

"I am happy to meet you, Miss Barrett. I understand from Fredrika that you are a writer, also," Edgar replied.

"Mr. Poe, I would not presume to call myself a writer standing in the company of one such as yourself. Say only that I dabble," Catherine returned. "'The Raven' was absolutely wonderful. Such power in the words that take the listener into the writer's mind. I should always fail when faced with genius such as yours."

"You are too kind, Miss, my thanks for the praise."

Just then Caroline joined the group and spoke, "Edgar, I have been trying to get Catherine to submit some of her poetry to your magazine. I think you would find it good enough to publish."

"By all means, Miss Barrett, do submit to the magazine, not all my readers like the somber timbre of my work. Yours might be just the light touch that it needs. I will look forward to discussing it with you further," Edgar enjoined.

"You are too kind, I will look and see if anything I have can be considered good enough for the public and let you know. But I warn you, they are a woman's musings only," Catherine answered.

"Let me decide if they are what we want or not. Just submit them," he said.

Several weeks later at home, Catherine was sitting in the conservatory writing at her desk. The day was stormy and the seas were rough far out on the horizon and she could hear the surf hitting the rocks far below her. The night before a storm had arrived and woke her in the night with the crashing of thunder and the lightning illuminating her room on the second floor. Her bedroom window faced the ocean and she could hear the roar of the surf even then as it rushed ever faster to the rocks on shore.

She had risen from her bed and grabbed a pen and paper and begun to write and now in the comparative quiet of the daylight hours, she looked back on what she had written. The storm was still blowing but now and then there was a respite and she could see the truth in what she had written. This perhaps might be good enough to show to Mr. Poe, she thought. She read it once again. She had entitled it "The Furies."

> It wakes me in the quiet night
> The wind's wild music raised in song
> And brings its pulsing piercing light
> To push back sleep the whole night long.
>
> Hail strikes like shrapnel on the roof
> Punctuated there with thunder
> And as if one needed further proof
> Searing points of light tear trees asunder.
>
> Rain lashing wild against the glass
> Like the sound of popping corn
> Staccato drumming coming fast
> While the wind blows its siren horn.
>
> And on and the forces war
> Until like soldiers in a battle spent
> The clouds swirl and split apart

To show a shaft of sunlight sent.

It's daylight now and there's cease-fire
As warring factions seek for peace
But those forces spinning ever higher
Must blow and wail until release.

See Earth tremble, white flag high
Waiting for the cool wind's steady hand
Waiting for the hot heads to pass by
Waiting for "all clear" upon the land.

Yes, perhaps, this was the one. She would take it to Mr. Poe's office this week and see if it would meet with his approval. Perhaps she'd take the others just in case he wanted to see them. She would not show them if he didn't like this one, there would be no point, for she was sure this was the best work she had done so far.

She arranged for transportation to the ferry and told her servant that she would not be overnight, to have a conveyance waiting for her there before the last ferry of the day. She hoped she would not be late, but she could not say for sure long she would be. There would be carriages for hire on the other side; she had seen the service before on the many occasions she had gone across while building the house.

When she arrived at the address that Caroline had given her, she saw an impressive building and inside many typesetters setting copy for the magazine's release. There on the second floor of the building were the offices of the editor and writers. Edgar's name was on his door. She approached and lightly rapped upon the door. "Come in," came the answer to her knock.

"Hello there," he said, "I had almost given up hope of hearing from you and here you are in the flesh indeed."

She blushed, for she hadn't any idea that he was really interested in her work. She had thought he was only being nice at the party, saying things that her friends expected him to say. She was amazed that he really did want to read her work.

"I am sorry I have not come before now, but it wasn't until just this week that I have written anything that I felt deserved to be published. It may not meet your expectations but here it is nevertheless." She thrust the paper on his desk.

"This is the only thing you have written that you believe is worth publishing?" he asked. "Surely there are more than this, my child, you can't have just started writing and produced only one work." He took a moment to read the poem that she had given him. "My word, child, this is not your first work! There is no way that this can come about in one try," he exclaimed.

"It's all right then, Mr. Poe?"

"It is more than all right, it is going into this month's issue. You have talent, perhaps you have genius. That remains to be seen, since you are young and just starting, but no matter you indeed have talent and I am always looking for talent. And please let us dispense with the Mr. Poe. My name is Edgar."

"Thank you so much, Edgar, I have always loved the written word and seeing my work in print will be the dream of my life."

"Say no more, we pay five cents per word, Miss, and the magazine will give you the cash or send a draft to your bank, whatever you prefer."

"A draft will be fine, though I wouldn't even care if you didn't pay me, to see it in print."

"Oh, but we must pay you, that is how we keep our talent." With that he took her poem to the downstairs typesetters and instructed them to find room in the next edition of the magazine for it. Catherine was ecstatic; she would be in print. What a wonderful place the United States was. She could own property, she could write, she could make her way. She was truly free here.

September 1846

It was her first salon, her first opening of the house to strangers, could she carry it off alone? Of course, she wouldn't be alone, Fredrika and Caroline would be here, and Edgar had said he would read for it. Dear Edgar, he had been so eager for her work all these past months and so attentive to her. But his time was not his own always, he might be abruptly called away to tend to Mrs. Poe. She knew that his wife was becoming more and more comatose and unaware of her surroundings, and she knew that Edgar suffered terribly for her. Catherine could remember Mamma's last days and could see the beginning of the end in the descriptions Edgar would tell. How horrible for him to see his lovely wife slipping away. She couldn't think about this now though, she must concentrate on the arrangements for the party tonight. Would there be enough port and claret, would the desserts and pastries be tempting to her guests. How did Fredrika do it?

There, the first carriage was pulling to the door, she was going to have to keep sending her coachman back and forth until all had arrived from the ferry. Poor man, she would have to give him a bonus for all the driving and work he would do tonight.

"Fredrika, how wonderful to have you in my home," Catherine called as she hurried to see to her guest's comfort.

"Catherine, you must give us a tour of this wonderful house of yours, perhaps even let me stay and see it in the daylight!" Fredrika exclaimed.

"You know you are welcome to stay as long as you like," Catherine said.

"Then you don't need to give me a tour, I will stay and see if in the daylight with you in the morning." Fredrika laughed.

"Who was with you in the carriage, Fredrika?"

"Only the Smiths and your editor." Fredrika smiled. And Catherine turned to see them approaching from the hall. Catherine stepped forward to give her hands to her friends and turned a special smile on Edgar.

"Welcome to my home, all of you." She smiled.

"Thank you, Cathy," Edgar returned, "it is a beautiful home and should be so as a setting to a beautiful jewel like you."

"Why, Edgar, how lovely of you, thank you," Cathy said.

"Now, everyone, eat and drink, while I welcome the rest of our friends. I shan't be long, but like you, Fredrika, I must see to everyone's welcome and comfort. Please excuse me."

The guests arrived one after another, until the drawing room and dining room were filled with people. The conservatory was set up for the entertainment and when the time had come for that to happen, Catherine rang a bell to call everyone to his or her seats. Edgar had the place of honor on the podium and had another gracious poem to read for them. As before they were spell bound, but upon finishing he let them clap and call their praise. A hush came upon the room as he raised his hands for silence. He looked at Catherine and said, "Cathy, please do us the honor of reading something for us from the many poems you have written."

"Yes, yes, Cathy, please give us a poem of your own," came the voices in the room.

"I have never performed before, but if it would please you, give me a moment." She crossed to her desk that had been moved to make room for the podium, and reaching in a drawer pulled a paper from it. She crossed the room to the podium that Edgar had vacated and looked at him in the seat that she had sat in. His eyes were smiling at her. She started to speak.

"'It is always darkest before the dawn.'
Someone said that a long time ago.
Who it was somehow I don't remember right now
Or maybe I never did know.

It's true enough though in the wee tiny hour
Just before the gray light shows through
There's nary a trace of tree, house, or flower
Can be seen in the fresh rising dew.

How is it that in the time before light
We can feel the presence so near?
The loved ones we knew, their forms pure and bright,
And behold them without any fear.

Are they just there behind the lids
Of our eyes fast closed in our sleep?
Promising never to leave us behind
Remembering the vows that they keep.

Are they the angels we heard of when young
That mothers would speak of to child?
Are they those mothers themselves who are sung
Of in ballads so meek and so mild?

No matter what, it's a comfort to know
There is something or someone waiting for me
When I close my eyes and my breath slows
And my soul starts its traveled road free.

"I call it 'Inside My Eyes,'" she said. The applause came again and again. She was uplifted that her contemporaries were impressed with her work. She had arrived.

The evening wore on as first this guest and then that guest toasted and cheered for them, but as all good things, this evening too had to end. The carriage was summoned and the guests were started back to the ferry. All

93

were gotten off the island in time with the exception of the Smiths, Edgar, and Frederika. By the time they had taken their leave the last ferry of the night had crossed not to return until morning. Catherine called her servants and had them make ready the guests' rooms for her guests. The house would not be empty tonight.

The next day after the salon, Catherine took her guests on a tour of the house and grounds. The air was brisk and cool and there was a hint of fall in the air. As the five of them walked along the cliff side, they could see the flocks of geese making Vs in the air over the mainland, getting ready for their winter migration. They strolled the grounds until time to return to the house to ready themselves for the ferry ride back to New York.

Walking them to the door, Edgar hung back and took Catherine's hands in his.

"Cathy, I think you should consider having your poems printed and bound in a book. If you allow them to just lie in a folder or a drawer, they may be lost for all time. Please consider what I have said. Your gift deserves to be safeguarded for the future generations."

Catherine looked intently at him, she felt that he was trying to tell her something important, but he said no more. Yes, she would consider it. She had been thinking about it herself. There was nothing to stop her, the money was there, she had enough poems now to make a book worthwhile, and she thought that perhaps her friends would enjoy a copy of their own to remember her by.

She bid her friends goodbye and returned to her room to rest.

The next week while Caroline was visiting, Catherine asked her to give her the names of some good printers and bookbinders. Caroline wondered at her interest but complied without question. With this information in hand, Catherine made her way into the city to talk with these people. She decided on one with whom she felt she could work, and having gathered all her works together in good order, she left them with the printer and asked that ten copies be printed and bound. What type of binding did she prefer? She thought a green leather would be good, and the title and author's name?

"The title should read, TIMELESS," she said, " that only on the cover." And for the spine they asked, "The same, except include my name."

"And that would be?
"Leave it blank for now," she answered.

CHAPTER EIGHT

September 18, 2001

Later that week, after refusals by both of her girls, they had this and that to do and could not be bothered with a dirty, old auction but they hoped she had a good time, Missy decided. It was up to her to go to the auction by herself, if she really wanted to go. She usually went to these things with Jeff or Jeff and the girls. It wouldn't be as much fun to go alone, perhaps she should call Elaine. But then she remembered, Elaine was out of town for the next couple of days.

So she grabbed her checkbook and purse and took off in the early morning hours to drive to the farm, which was some way from her home. When she arrived, there were already many cars parked haphazardly around and she hurried to the cashier to pick up a number. She wandered around the plank tables set on sawhorses in the grass looking first at one box and then another until she came to the boxes filled with old books. There were spellers written in the early 1900s and primers for children to read from and old bibles and underneath looking very dusty and dog-eared was an old book of poetry. It was a small volume covered in green leather. The title on the front was almost rubbed away, and she could just make it out. *Timeless* was the name on the front. Hmm, who is the author? she wondered, it wasn't on the front. But there on the spine was the author's name. Catherine Aurora Barrett-Poe. No one she recognized. Perhaps she was interested, perhaps not. She would have to see how much the box went for.

The bidding was long and the items went for this price and that price and finally they approached the table where the boxes of books were stacked. Missy had almost left a number of times but as they reached the table she noticed that there were fewer bidders at this time. Those that had stayed had evidently their eye on the same box she had seen. The auctioneer raised the box aloft and began the bidding.

"What am I bid, for this box of books?" he asked.

Someone across the table from Missy had a bid. "$5.00." Missy held up her number for the auctioneer to notice her.

"$5.50."

"$6.00."

"$6.50."

"$10.00," came the other bidder.

"$15.00," Missy answered.

The auctioneer looked across the table at the other bidder. But he had suddenly disappeared. He looked back at Missy and cried, "Going once, going, twice, sold, to the young lady for $15.00."

Missy hurried to the cashier with her box of books to write her check. As she was coming out a man stopped her and asked, "I noticed you won the bid on those books, are you interested in all of them or just one special one."

"Oh, I am interested in all of the them, I'm sorry," Missy answered and she hurried to her car to carry her treasures away.

She looked again at the old spellers and primers and wondered what the man had been so interested in, and then her eye caught the other book. The one that had interested her, and now she remembered the title was the same one Jeff had told her about a week ago. She had forgotten until now about the woman who wanted the research done. She would take a closer look at it this evening. Jeff had a late meeting with clients and she would be by herself, she would read it then.

When her dinner was over and the lights in the library turned to comfortable reading levels, Marissa pulled the small book out of the box and looked at it. It had obviously been handled and read a lot, the gold leaf on the cover of the book was almost rubbed away as if someone had held it close many times. The pages were dog-eared and there were notations in the margins. There was no copyright number on the flyleaf but only the words "Limited Edition" and the date of publication. Who had published this book and where had it been all this time? The pages were yellowed with age and the writer's initials were printed at the top of every page in faded green ink outlined with shamrocks or Old Irish design or something.

Marissa began to read and it was as if she was reading her own work. The poetry was fluid and filled with desires and hopes and day-to-day happenings of the writer's life. It was like stepping into another's life and experiencing their thoughts and dreams. Wouldn't Jeff be surprised when she presented him with her very own copy of the book that they had been discussing just that very week? She was musing on these facts, when the doorbell buzzed.

She wondered who could be there. Jeff shouldn't be getting home yet and the girls didn't check in with her anymore now that they lived away from home.

She rose from the armchair she had been sitting in and went to the front window to peek onto the porch.

At her door stood a policeman politely waiting for her to open the door.

"Yes, officer," Marissa said as she pulled the door open wide, "what can I do for you?"

"I am sorry to be the bearer of bad news, mam, but there has been an accident. I need for you to get a wrap and come with me."

"Oh, my heavens, who has had an accident, which one of my girls has had an accident?"

"It isn't your girls, Mrs. Delclare, it's your husband and he has been taken to County General."

"Oh no, is he hurt bad? Just a moment, while I get my coat and purse."

"I'm afraid so. We'd best go now."

Marissa could not think, she could not even imagine what could have happened. Jeff wasn't even supposed to be on the road yet. Why had he left the meeting early? How bad was he hurt? Why wouldn't anyone tell her anything? They drove with sirens wailing through the night carrying her to his side. When she arrived in the emergency area, she heard the dread words from the doctors: "We have done all we can do, now it is up to God."

Jeff lay swathed in bandages in intensive care. He looked almost like a mummy, he was so bandaged. It seemed that the meeting had ended early and he was hurrying home to be with her when a drunk driver ran a red light and caused the smash up of Jeff's car. The car veered off the road before jumping a curb and smashing into a building. The other driver had left the scene. Jeff was unconscious when the paramedics arrived and the fire department was needed to extricate him from his car. He had called her name once, during the ride to the hospital and then lapsed again into a state of semi-consciousness and now could not be wakened. The bandages were for the cuts and contusions he had suffered. They would heal but would Marissa ever hear his voice again?

Now during the days and nights of hospital call, Marissa would tumble into bed exhausted at night and reach for him, but the empty pillow only brought her grief closer to her. She would talk to him for hours, and then, when the things of conversation waned she began to bring books to read to him. Jeff always loved everything the printed word had to offer. She would read newspapers and magazines and travel brochures to him hoping that each day something would ignite the spark that would wake him.

During those days when Marissa was so often gone from home, her girls would leave their jobs and families and come and straighten up or prepare a meal for her to eat when she returned. Her daughters would spell her at the hospital when she would steal away for a few moments' rest and would always say on her return, "No change, Mom."

Marissa would nod and sit down and begin to read again or talk again and even sometimes to sing to Jeff to try to spark the fire of life and reach him in his unending sleep. The doctors shook their heads and spoke of nursing care facilities and other things but she steadfastly held to the belief that Jeff would be coming back.

Then one night when she got home, she looked for the box that she had been looking at when the news came that Jeff had been injured. Where had the girls put it? She hadn't been home for any length of time for so long, she had forgotten all about it. She called the daughter who had cleaned up the day after the accident happened and asked her where she had put the things in the library. She informed her that she supposed that they had belonged on the shelf so she alphabetized them and put them on the shelves. Marissa looked along the shelves until she found the little book that she had been reading that night. The writer had caught her own thoughts so well; perhaps this was the book to read to Jeff.

The next day when she got to the hospital, the doctor stopped her in the hall.

"Mrs. Delclare, I am sorry to have to tell you this but we are going to have to move Jeff to another facility in a day or two. We need the bed space here for people we can help. We can't do anything else for your husband."

"I understand," she said and walked into her husband's room to sit beside him.

He looked so peaceful, like he had just fallen asleep. The bandages were gone now and he was looking a little pale from being in bed, but otherwise he looked like her Jeff. How long could he keep looking like that lying in bed? she wondered. She lowered her head on the bed and said a silent prayer.

"Please, God let this book be the one. Let me find one poem in here that will be the one." She began to read. Her voice was strong and low and the cadence of the poetry was like music. She leaned forward to the bed and grasped Jeff's hand with a gentle pressure. Suddenly she remembered the poem she had written Jeff before they were married. Surely he would remember that one, surely that one would be the one of all the poetry and all the books that would be in his subconscious. She began to recite it even though it had been many years since she had written it.

> I may not live a long, long time
> But I have known you,
> So time has lost its meaning
> And all my life a moment true.
>
> My dreams would cease for me
> When you are no longer near
> My world of gossamer thread collapse
> And here I'm left with only a tear.
>
> The strength and fiber of my love,
> Such shall never come to me again,
> Draws its breath from love for you
> That knows neither how nor when
>
> And even as the mysteries of life
> The reasons why I came here free,
> I can't explain or yet convey,
> Through life to walk this way to thee.
>
> In God I trust to answer all
> I pray your love is mine to stay
> And I'm content with blessings small
> Forever, 'til I go my way.

Her tears were flowing and she could hardly get the last line out, but then she felt the gentle pressure of his fingers and she looked from the page to see his eyes smiling at her from the bed.

"Oh Jeff, I knew you would remember, I knew you were there, only just on the other side of this world." Marissa sobbed and covered his face with kisses.

January 1847

Edgar sat beside the bed of his wife and held her hand. She was so weak now that she could hardly draw breath. He hated to see her suffer so but could not reconcile the pain he would feel on losing her. Why couldn't she have the great health of Catherine? The young woman simply sparkled with youth and vigor. Why couldn't his Virginia be as she? It was not fair that she could slip from his grasp so soon. He couldn't countenance it.

He picked up the pen and pad beside his chair, and while she slept on fitfully, he penned some new verses for her. If only she could wake and read them and be restored to him. If only she could attend the salons that he frequented to fill their purse, and hear him read. She would surely applaud as loudly as the whole company. His Virginia, he had loved her all his life. Why was she leaving him in pain?

His thoughts grew ever darker and more morose. Perhaps he should just end it all with her, for life would be too horrible to attend without her. But God forbids that avenue and he knew that his sweet Virginia was headed straight to the bosom of heaven, he could not circumvent God to join her before the deity ordained. Were there no bright days ahead for him? Were there no hopes to cling to then? What would he do without his sweet Virginia?

February 1847

Catherine pulled her robe around her and headed for the downstairs. The maid had awakened her with a troubled knock on the door.

"There is someone to see you, mam, and they said it was important." Who could it be at this hour of the morning, it was barely past 5:00 a.m. There, in the hall, stood her friend. Caroline rushed to her with her hair askew; she had been driven in the wind.

"Caroline, what are you doing here at this hour? Has something happened to Captain Smith?"

"Oh, Catherine, I just got the news. Edgar is in a terrible state. He is half crazy with drink."

"Why, what has happened?" Catherine asked but she thought she knew the answer before she got it.

"Mrs. Poe has gone to her reward and the poor man is beside himself with grief. She died yesterday and was entombed today and he immediately started drinking and has kept at it all day and all night. His friends fear for his life, that he may do something terrible."

"Perhaps I can help. Where is he? I will have the coach readied and bring him here. He needs watching and a quiet place to leave his anger. I think I can understand how he is feeling, abandoned and lost."

"If anyone can reach him, it would be you. You both have always seemed to speak the same language."

"Come, rest yourself, and I will get dressed and give the servants orders to have a room ready for him when we return. You must get back home and care for your husband. I will take care of Edgar. We will be good company for one another here."

The two women departed the house within the hour and took the ferry into New York. They parted company at Caroline's house and Catherine went to the last place Caroline knew him to be. He had left that establishment and made for his office. They said she would probably find him there. Catherine bade the coachman drive her to the office and when she arrived she found the printing area in disarray and the lights burning above in the office. Climbing the stairs, she could hear the sound of cursing and Edgar's voice crying out for mercy.

"Edgar, may I come in?" she called. "I have come to take you home."

"Come in at your peril, for I am not in a very civil mood tonight or today or whatever time it is in this damnable world."

"Oh, Edgar, do not behave so with me, I have come to take you home," she said again.

"I have no home, no wife, no life. Heaven has stolen her from me."

"Now come with me and let us reason together on this, perhaps tomorrow will find you in a better disposition. Please, I beg of you, do not make my hasty trip to town in vain. Come with me and rest your head upon the pillows in my house."

He looked at her with bloodshot eyes and haggard face, his clothes stained with the drink of the past hours on him and submitted to her gaze. With a cry, he threw himself on her breast and began to sob anew.

"Now, now, Edgar, it will be all right, come now, do not worry yourself so." And so she led him sobbing to the coach and into the night to her home at Seacliff.

November 2001

Jeff's recovery was to be slow and steady and the day Missy brought him home from the hospital was truly a day for celebration. She had taken special pains to fix an extra special dinner for him and the candles burned brightly over the dining table set with all the silver and crystal that they both enjoyed. It was over their after-dinner aperitif that Missy brought up the accident and the events that surrounded it. She had feared talking about it before now, so great was her dread of tumbling Jeff back into the abyss of unconsciousness that she had recovered him from. Now having him at home, safe and sound, if not completely recovered, gave her the strength to bring up that night.

"Jeff," Missy asked, "why were you returning home early that night? I hadn't expected you until much later. You usually call before you start out, why did you change your routine?"

"I had been with the client up until the time I got your phone call, and when I heard what was obviously distress in your voice, I hurried home as quickly as I could."

"My phone call? What do you mean my phone call? I didn't call! I had been sitting here reading a new book of poetry that I had picked up at the auction when the doorbell buzzed and the police told me about the accident."

Jeff looked at Missy intently.

"You didn't call? Are you sure, because I could have sworn it was your voice. The woman on the phone was sobbing and calling for me to hurry and come home, something terrible was happening. I just knew it was you."

"I don't understand, who could have called you and left such a message and why, for what reason?"

"I didn't either, that is why I was sure it was you. I rushed to my car and started home, when someone in another car came out of a side street and I swerved to miss him and then I don't remember another thing until I woke listening to you recite your poem to me."

"Oh, my darling, how horrible for you. Well, at least now you are home safe and sound."

"You mentioned that you were reading a new book when the policeman came."

"Yes, the book of poetry that I had been reading that night had the same title as the one you told me about at the publishing company and I wondered if it was the same author. I have it here on the library shelf in case you felt like looking at it when you got home."

Marissa crossed from the dining room into the library and returned with the small book. There it lay on the table, worn and well used, with the gold leaf of the title rubbed thin as though someone had held and caressed it many times. The pages were yellowed and smudged and some were obviously read over and over again because the book automatically fell open to those pages when it lay open on the table.

Jeff picked it up and looked at the author's name. Yes, it was the same author. It seemed to be the same book. He would have to check into this with the woman who wanted the research done on it when he returned to work. But that would have to wait until he was able to return to the office and the doctors had warned him against rushing back to work for a while.

He would call the office tomorrow though and have them send the copy he had there to his home and compare the two books. Perhaps there was something he was missing here. He looked again at the copyright page, no copyright number, just the words, "Limited Edition." Copy one of ten. But there was a notation handwritten on the inside cover. "Jonathan, when your father comes, give him this book. Love, Mother." Not unusual to find notes from givers of books to those they had been given to. Hmm, somehow there was something different here, but he couldn't quite put his mental finger on it. He would wait to see what the other copy said.

"Missy," he said, "can I borrow your copy for a few days, I want to compare it with the other copy at work."

"You aren't going to work yet, are you?"

"No, I will call them and have the copy sent over tomorrow."

"Okay, but now I think you have had enough of an evening, so it's off to bed with you!"

"Only if I'm snuggled next to you, young lady. I have had enough nights without you."

"Try and keep me out."

Marissa wandered through the house turning out the lights and straightening up the dinner things as Jeff went up the stairs to get ready for bed. She picked up the small volume again from where Jeff had laid it on the library table and leafed through it. Yes, it was well used and often read, but the poetry seemed innocent enough. What could it be that had Jeff interested in her copy? There were handwritten notes in the margins but only those showing interests in some verse or other of the poem. And there was the notation in the front cover, that she had seen, but just a message from a mother to her son. Nothing extraordinary about that. She remembered the man who had bid against her at the auction now, and his interest in the box of books. Who was he? What did he have to do with the poetry book, or for that matter, with Jeff's accident? She would definitely be doing some research of her own and the sooner the better. She took a pen and paper and jotted down the exact spelling of the title and the author's name. Tucking it into her purse, she snapped the final light switch and climbed the steps to bed.

Outside in the darkened night, a car parked across the lane from the Delclares' home sat still and quiet as the occupant watched the lights in the house across the way go out one by one. Then an engine sputtered to life and the vehicle slowiy moved off into the night.

CHAPTER NINE

February 1847

The morning dawned cold and gray and it matched Edgar's mood; he was hung over and miserable. Why had Catherine brought him here? He was no fit company for a young woman right now. He must take his leave from her as soon as he was able. The servant knocked at his door gently. "Sir, Miss Catherine has sent a tea tray to you, she will join you shortly but please take some nourishment," the maid called while endeavoring to get the door open. She balanced the tray neatly, carrying it to a table before the fireplace. Then as she began filling the hearth with fresh wood, a warming crackle began to fill the room. She glanced at him still and quiet on the bed and turning slowly away left the room.

Edgar pulled a robe that lay across the bed over his arms and walked unsteadily to the fire. He felt a hundred years old instead of his thirty-eight years. Where was the reason for living anymore? Where was the desire to make a way in the world? Where were the golden dreams of his youth? He was desolate and wanted no food to nourish his body.

He sat before the tray and the fire and brooded on these things growing ever more despondent, when a soft knock at the door as it slowly opened announced another visitor. Catherine came slowly into the room dressed in a morning gown of sunny yellow. She looked like a daffodil just picked from the garden. He couldn't help but make the comparison.

"Cathy, your hospitality is gracious but I fear that nourishment is the last thing I want today. Please desist your efforts on my behalf. I am not worth saving. I couldn't save her, and I don't want to be saved, either," Edgar blurted.

"Edgar, please don't worry about offending me or upsetting me, I understand completely how you feel," Cathy returned.

"Cathy, you can't possibly know how I feel. You are young and, as yet, have not been either in love or loved by one, so how can you know the feelings of loss that I am suffering?" he said.

"Edgar, we are friends and what I share with you now must go no further, for my very life here at Seacliff would be forfeit were the knowledge I am about to give you go any further. But long ago, I, too, was abandoned by the ones who should be the last to abandon you. So I have lived my entire life with that feeling of loss," Cathy whispered.

Edgar looked into her eyes and saw the truth of what she said. He listened as the story unfolded. Now he understood why she had seemed familiar and why her talent sprang so naturally from her. Here, indeed, was someone who would understand the grief of losing those she loved before ever really knowing them. Here was the illegitimate daughter of Elizabeth Barrett in the flesh. Her travel to another country far away from the familiar she had grown up with must have been a horrible experience, but she had put her chin up and struck out to make her way. Here was a strength that he did not have, but then she was young and the young are sure of their invincibility. Hadn't he been sure of his when he was that age? At the last, he drew from her the strength he needed and took the tea and pastries from the tray.

They walked abroad in the chilling air that day, along the cliffs and in the mists and talked of their lives, and how they had each had a goal. Edgar wondered where his goal was now. This girl, for she was still a girl, she had a goal, to survive and make a home for herself here. What could he do now that Virginia was gone?

Edgar couldn't seem to see ahead, there was a fog in his mind that wouldn't lift.

Catherine found herself drawn to him in his sadness and wanted so to bring him back to the land of the living. She saw his genius wasted and him struggling to fight the moods and sadness of his loss. What could she do for him? He had done everything for her, why couldn't he see that she could be to him what he needed? She had borne her feelings for him silently till now, but all obstacles were lifted, surely he would take the gift of her love. She continued through the days to listen to him pour out the virtues of Virginia and she waited.

When Edgar had been a visitor at her house for some weeks, her friend Caroline called to see what progress he was making. She confided to Catherine that she could see no change for the better, other than the fact that his drinking had seemed to slow in her presence. "Catherine," she said, "you must realize what people may be saying about you with Edgar here and you a single woman."

"Caroline, how can you say such a thing to me, when you can surely see how much he suffers for her yet," Catherine cried.

"Yes, that is true, I can see it, but I must say that there will be talk. I will go and see Fredrika and suggest that she come and stay a while with you, while Edgar is here." Caroline said, "That may stop the tongues wagging."

"Let them wag, if that is all the better friends they are, but if you worry so, send Fredrika for a stay and she can judge what protection I may need."

That very evening at their dinner Catherine mentioned to Edgar that perhaps Fredrika would be coming for a stay to help cheer him. It seemed that her company alone was not enough to bring him out of his sorrows.

Edgar crossed to her side and took her hands; he looked closely at her face and beheld there tears gathering in her eyes. Surely this child did not pine for him herself. Surely, he wasn't the cause of those tears. He was an old man after all. She needed youth to call to her spirit. But he held her hands even so.

"Are you distressed because you have not succeeded in raising me from my grief, or are you distressed that now we will no longer have the moments spent together here alone?" he asked.

"Both things are true," she said and wiped at her eyes with her hands.

"Don't cry, child, I have never been able to abide tears. They will destroy me completely." He pulled her to him and held her tight against his chest. He could feel her tremble within his grasp. Her heart was beating wildly and he held her back to see the pulse throbbing in her neck. Then slowly, he leaned down to touch her lips with his. The lightning tore through the house as though a storm had rolled and roiled outside. The grip of passion soared into his veins and he held her tight against him. She grasped him back and held him tightly and when again he released her, she lowered his head to kiss him too. The dinner things were forgotten as they climbed the stairs to his bed. He would take her there and spare the servants gossip.

It didn't matter that he was so much older than she. It didn't matter that he was taking without any hope of returning the gift of youth to her. All that mattered was the burning in his loins that once again spoke to him of life instead of death, and she brought this gift to him in all its glory. All night he savored her glorious youth and when the first birdsong was heard he rushed her to her room to rest and wake with the others. He would invent some story for the bedclothes, it would have to suffice, and he would be away before Fredrika came. For he knew to stay would compromise her more. Oh, if he were only ten years younger, he would claim and fight for her to keep her for himself. But she deserved better than a used-up old man.

Catherine slept the sleep of the dead until the cock had crowed in the far off fields more than once and the house was stirring. She felt delicious like a pastry that had been tasted and found desirable. Her world was complete now; she and Edgar would have everything she could provide. She would give him a magazine of his own, not just one that he worked for. They would be supremely happy. She knew now why God had sent her here.

At breakfast she found him strangely distant, and she wondered whether she was the only one who had been affected by the night's wonder.

"Catherine, I must go back to the city. You have shown me that it is pointless to grieve so and I need to be about the job of living again. I will return when I have tidied up my affairs." He couldn't look her straight in the eye; she was so beautiful this morning and his resolution would fail him if he looked into those eyes again. He must be away from her for her own good.

"Edgar, send me word when you will be back and I will send a coach for you," Catherine said, not wanting to press him for further explanation. Surely she must trust him and take him at his word. She was dismayed that he would leave so soon, but she would wait, he was a man and he had to come to the knowledge of his feelings for her on his own. She could not make him love her; she could only love him and hope he would love her back someday.

November 8, 2001

The following morning after Marissa had finished serving his breakfast, Jeff went to the library and picked up the small poetry book and began looking at it more closely. Yes, it certainly looked like the other book, though the other book wasn't quite as well used. That one had looked as though it had just come off the printer's floor, like it had been kept closely guarded and treasured though in a different way. Yes, he would have to get the other copy here to really study them. He would call his office right away and have it sent over.

He dialed his secretary, "Donna, this is Jeff. Yes, I am home and doing better every day. No, I don't think I will be in to the office for a while yet, but I do have a favor to ask of you. Remember the book, the poetry book we were going to research for the woman? Title of *Timeless*. You do. Good, have that book sent over to the house for me, will you? I might at least do some work from here at home if possible. What? Oh, you will have to find it.

Well, what happened to it? Oh, well then as soon as you lay your hands on it, send it along. Okay. Also, you know the other project I was working on for Marissa? Is it finished yet? Oh good, send me a copy of that also. There's what? Well, stick it inside the books and send it all over."

Jeff hung the telephone up and leaned back in his chair. That was strange, the woman no longer wanted to do research on it. Well, now he wanted to do the research, there was something funny going on here and he intended to find out what it was.

November 11, 2001

It was some time later in the week that the messenger finally arrived with the brown package containing the book that he had been waiting for. Along with the package was a letter addressed to his wife from someone who had written to her with her married name of Feinstein at the publishing company and the other book that Donna had said she would send. That was strange. Marissa hadn't worked at the publishing company for many years. Why would anyone write to her there? He would have to give her the letter and get her reactions to it. After dinner would be a good time to go over it with her. She was away now with friends for lunch, but he would ask her about it then.

Meanwhile Marissa was doing a little research of her own. She had taken the poetry book's title and author's name and was sitting in the restaurant with her friends having lunch trying to figure the best way to start her research. She asked her oldest friend, Elaine, what she thought about the whole thing. Elaine suggested that she start at the copyright office and see if the work had, indeed, ever been copyrighted. Then check the author's name against the records of literary journals and library historical records, maybe even look at genealogical records on the name. All good suggestions, she decided, she would head for the library right after lunch.

Elaine looked up and saw a face she thought she knew and mentioned to Marissa, "Isn't that someone we know, he certainly looks a lot like someone I used to know or have seen before. I just can't put a name to a face."

Marissa glanced up from her musings and saw the face of a man that she thought she had seen before too, but where.

"He does look familiar."

Oh well, perhaps it would come to her.

"I best finish this lunch and get about my business," she said, "Jeff will be wondering where I am, if I'm gone too long."

She gathered up her purse and keys and said goodbye to her friends. As she left the restaurant to return to her car, she had the feeling that she was being followed. It persisted even though she didn't see anyone.

May 1847

Catherine and Fredrika were taking their tea in the conservatory and were enjoying the warm sunshine which promised to herald a day of warm weather. May was beginning to be all it had promised in the beginning of the month. Theresa, the maid, came to announce that a messenger had arrived from the printers with a bundle. Catherine thanked her and hurried to the front hall to receive him.

"Miss Catherine Barrett," the man inquired.

"Yes, I'm Catherine Barrett, how can I help you?"

"I'm delivering the books that you ordered. Please sign here on the receipt."

"Thank you," she said. She signed the sheet of paper that he held out and then he turned and left her home. She watched as he drove away. Then she took the bundle and handed it to the maid.

"Please see that this is put in my closet in my room. I will open it later." She returned to sit with Fredrika.

"Anything important, Catherine?"

"No, just a package delivered. I have taken care of it for now. Let's continue our conversation."

It had been more than a month since Edgar had left and she had expected to receive some word from him by now. Perhaps Fredrika could give her some inkling of what was happening. Out here on Long Island at Seacliff, she didn't hear the gossip of the city and she would not go again to him; she had literally thrown herself at him once, she would not do so again.

"Are you still having salons?"

"Not so many since the weather began to turn. Everyone has been enjoying the spring colors and so many have been out in the woods and along the streams capturing the countryside on canvas, and the writers are working harder than ever. I expect that now that the cold weather has finished, we will start to come together again. Why do you ask?"

"I just wondered, I hadn't heard of any and I have been preoccupied here at Seacliff. I must pay a visit to Caroline, it has been a month or more since I have seen her and it is not like us to be apart so much."

"Oh, I thought you had heard and that is why I hadn't mentioned it before now, but Caroline is expecting and has been feeling a little under the weather these past weeks. I imagine once that passes, she will pay a call on you. But do not tell her I told you, it will ruin her surprise," Fredrika said.

"Oh, how wonderful for her, I know that she and the captain have long wanted a child, I imagine she is beside herself with happiness."

"Yes, I am sure what you say is true, but right now the facts of the pregnancy are weighing heavily on her stomach. She is having trouble keeping anything down. But she is strong and I am sure will come to rights eventually."

Catherine herself sometimes didn't feel well in the mornings, but she was right as rain by lunch. She could understand Caroline's discomfort. Should she confide in Fredrika what she pondered to herself? Perhaps not at this time, it should be Caroline whom she should talk to. The two women continued to gossip and talk through until supper when they took their leave of each other for an early bedtime. Fredrika wanted to catch the early ferry to the city; she was not long for New York as she was planning to continue her journey to Europe before returning home to her native land of Sweden.

Catherine said goodbye to her the next morning and immediately readied herself to follow after on a later ferry. Best not to raise any questions about her visit to the city. She found the address of the physician that her maid had mentioned, and paid a visit to his office.

"Yes, Mrs. Poe, it was as you ascertained. You are indeed going to have a baby. Before the end of the year, I expect."

Catherine was overjoyed, a child of hers and Edgar's, what a wonderful gift from God. She couldn't wait to tell him. First she would see Caroline and share the news with her. She had been her greatest friend. She would understand the passions that had overwhelmed her that night with Edgar. Surely he would hurry to her now, surely he would love the woman who carried his child.

She bade the cabby drive her to Captain Smith and Caroline's home. A surprise visit would be welcomed, she was sure. Especially when she heard the news that they would spend their confinement together. Catherine knocked on the door. The maid answered and showed to her to the parlor and went to fetch Caroline.

Caroline did indeed look ill, Catherine thought as soon as she saw her

112

enter the room. "Catherine, how wonderful to see you. And how are Edgar and Fredrika?"

Catherine released the hands she had been holding.

"Fredrika is fine, but about Edgar I have no idea. I have not seen him for a month."

"Oh, I was sure that he had gone to you, since he closed his office and disappeared."

"Disappeared, what do you mean disappeared?"

"I mean, that he closed his office one day and no one has seen him since."

Catherine sat heavily on the parlor sofa. He had left her without a word. He did not want her love or her affection. What was she to do? She carried his child, she was sure that he would marry her. Why had he left? What was there to be done about it? She looked at Caroline with an immense grief on her face and then crumpled in a heap.

Sometime later she awakened with Caroline pressing cool cloths against her cheeks. "Catherine, Catherine, wake up, wake up," Caroline was nervously calling. "What troubles you, child?"

"Oh, Caroline, I have been such a fool. I thought that he cared for me. I thought that I could rescue him. I have only myself to blame for driving him away. Now I have brought another like myself into the world."

"Catherine, what are you saying, another like yourself?"

"Only another unwanted child whose father doesn't want it or the mother."

"Are you saying that you are going to have a child also and that Edgar is the father?" Caroline was dismayed.

"Whose else could it be, I have only had contact with him all my time in this country. I truly thought that he cared for me, he said he would return."

"We must find where he has gone and tell him, we must bring him back to face his responsibilities."

"Never! I don't want him if he doesn't love me. I won't have him unless he comes of his own free will. Do not search for him. My child and I will wait for him to come back to us. Promise me you will say nothing about this, only that I am in seclusion and nothing more."

"I promise, but I think you are wrong not to tell him about the child."

"Perhaps, but this is the way it is to be," Catherine said. Again, she stiffened her heart and went home to face the world alone.

CHAPTER TEN

November 11, 2001, 3:00 p.m.

The library was still and hushed, as though all the many words that lingered there on all those pages were shushed, waiting for a human mouth to utter them. Martha sat at the marble-topped counter leafing through pages of books looking for signs of damage as Marissa walked toward her area. She paused to observe the woman coming toward her, a woman in her later years dressed in classic romantic style with lace at her throat and wrists but with a trim suit which scarcely hid her good figure. She crossed to the counter and opened the leather bag, fishing in the bottom for a piece of paper with some information scribbled on it. The paper was thrust forward. "Excuse me, please, Martha, can you help me find the genealogical and library of congress section, I need to do some research."

The librarian looked at the paper and then again at her friend.

"Sure, just follow me, I'll show you where they are." They walked together down several aisles of books and finally stopped at the next to the last row of bookshelves. Martha pulled several volumes from the shelves and handed them to Marissa.

"These may be of some help to you. If you need anything else, Missy, just call me."

"Thank you." She carried the volumes to one of the library reading tables and sat down to read. The volume on genealogy seemed to be the place to start, and she started first with the name of Poe, it was, of course, familiar for all poets were familiar with Edgar Allen Poe's works but not with a Catherine Barrett-Poe. She looked into the name Browning and saw a family tree for Elizabeth Barrett Browning and Robert Browning.

There was only one child, a boy, listed for them, as they were not married until 1846. The dates for birth and death for Elizabeth Barrett Browning was 1806 to 1861, and for Robert Browning were 1812 to 1889. Next she checked Edgar Allen Poe's birth and death dates and there it showed the dates of

1809 to 1849. So where did Catherine Aurora Barrett Poe come from? Was she the daughter of Elizabeth but not Robert? Why was she carrying the name Poe?

Catherine would have to have been born in England. Poe was a United States citizen. How would they have met? So many questions and then, even more, when she found no record of the works of Catherine Aurora Barrett-Poe ever recorded in the Library of Congress Copyright Records. Who was Catherine Aurora Barrett and where did she come from? Did Catherine have a secret marriage with Edgar that she did not want anyone to know about or did she just take his name for some reason? What happened to Catherine?

Did the poetry that Edgar wrote in such poems as "A Dream Within a Dream," "To One In Paradise," and "The Haunted Palace" really have to do with Catherine all this time? If this were true, why the copies of her works would be worth millions, especially since there were only a few copies. She seemed to remember that there were only ten copies of the book printed according to the flypage and the date of publication had been 1847. She hurried to copy the dates of these people and her thoughts on it on paper for Jeff to read later when she got home. She felt she knew the reason for the interest in the book now, but what she was to find on arriving home both shocked and infuriated her.

November 11, 2001, 5:30 p.m.

Marissa opened the door to the garage and pulled the car inside. The house was quiet as a tomb. No one inside was moving. She opened the trunk of the car and pulled out her research folder full of notes that she had placed there on leaving the library.

"Jeff, are you awake?" She opened the kitchen door, raising her voice to reach him in the bedroom if he had gone for nap. No answer. She snapped on the lights in the living room and found the entire house turned upside down. Books and magazines were tossed everywhere, cushions pulled off the couches and chairs, and drawers hung crazily open and the contents spilled from them onto the floor. Jeff was nowhere to be seen. What could have happened to him? She rushed to the phone to call 911 when she saw the light on the answering machine pulsing; someone had left a message. Oh, please, let it be Jeff.

Pushing the button on the machine, she sat on the floor and concentrated on the voice on the tape.

"Just give me the book and nothing will happen to him!" the voice uttered. "I will give you instructions on where and when to drop it, you will get your husband back when I get the book and not before. Don't call the police or you will be sorry." Marissa listened while her blood ran cold and the skin on the back of her neck began to crawl. She didn't have the book; she had left it with Jeff. What had he done with it? Oh, heavens, what was she going to do now?

She called Elaine and poured out the story to her. Elaine said to hang up and she would be right over to help her look. She was so distraught; she didn't know where to start. Why did she have the suspicion that she had heard the voice before? Who could do such a thing and for what reason? Was it because the books were so valuable? That had to be it. No one could be this sinister for any other reason. She had to find that book. If Jeff had discovered something, surely he would have left her a note or something. She moved to the library where she was sure Jeff would have been working when the individual surprised him. Or perhaps he was sleeping peacefully and was drugged and taken before the search. If that were the case he would have left her a note before his nap. Now where was a secret place that he might put a note that only she would think to look? It looked as though the whole house was torn apart, but that was not entirely true, it was only the downstairs that was disturbed as though the offender was surprised and had to stop and leave the premises before he completely finished the job. Then he must have secreted Jeff somewhere so that no one would see him while he ransacked the place. Where would he have put him?

Just then the doorbell buzzed and she rushed to open the door. It was Elaine and she folded Marissa into her arms as she began to speak in a torrent of words.

"Elaine, you must help me think what Jeff would have done with that book, it means his life. The man obviously does not have it and that means it must be here somewhere or else Jeff has done something with it." Marissa stared at her with fear in her eyes.

"Marissa, what do you mean, it means his life?"

"I mean, it means his life, if I can't find that book. The man was quite clear about that. He means to have the books, or he will kill Jeff," she sobbed.

Elaine just shook her head. "I don't understand what there can be about a book that means so much that a man would be killed over it. And what do you mean by books? Why would there be more than one? Who is this man anyway?"

"I don't know who the man is, but I think," Marissa said, "that this book or collection of books is very rare and are written by the secret wife or lover of Edgar Allan Poe. That would make them very interesting reading and very old, and since they are unpublished insofar as they were not put out for general readership, everyone would want to own one. So in that respect, they would be worth millions. I bought one at an auction and Jeff had another come into his hands recently during a research search."

"Wow, are you sure?"

"Well, as sure as I can be without asking the people involved, and since they have been dead for a long time, there is no hope of asking them, but the dates fit and it is the only thing that makes sense."

"Were there any other messages on the tape?"

"What? Oh, I forgot to check, I called you before listening to all the messages. The only one I heard was the message about Jeff being kidnapped and I haven't heard the rest yet." She turned back to the answering machine and began to listen to the other messages that were recorded. Pretty soon she heard Jeff's voice talking to her from the speaker.

"Honey, I got my copy of that book that we were talking about from the office today and there is a letter for you along with it. Remind me to give it to you when I see you. I have put all the books in…." The tape ran out of time, there was no more to the message. What had he done with the books?

Elaine looked at Marissa and said, "Marissa, you have got to call the police, they will be able to check for fingerprints, and maybe even have a lead on any suspicious things connected to the accident. You have got to call them right now, before too much time goes by. Have you called the kids yet?"

"No, I didn't want to worry them yet. If we find the book and get Jeff back, everything will be fine. You know how emotional Sandy and Willow get. And Leslie and Leon are just as bad only in a quieter, more desperate way. No, I won't tell them until I absolutely have to. Anyway, Leon is on the other side of the world. He couldn't do anything but pray. I'll call him for that help, of course, but first I need to do everything I can from here," Marissa replied.

"Well, call the police right now, while I'm here," Elaine said.

"Yes, I will, but I just kept hoping I would find the book and when he called I could give it to him and this would all be over. I'll call them right now." She pulled the telephone book out of the desk drawer and looked up the number. As she dialed the phone, she was thinking of all the things that she and Jeff had planned to do now that he was home from the hospital and feeling better. Poor Jeff, she could only feel a stab at her heart when she wondered at what kind of treatment he was getting. He was still so weak from being in bed for so long. The voice on the other end of the line startled her back to reality,

"Hello, this is the Sheriff's Department, how can I help you?"

"I would like to speak to someone in charge of missing persons, please," Marissa replied.

A man's voice came on the line and asked, "Who is missing and how long have they been gone?"

"I really don't know what time he disappeared, but my husband has been kidnapped and I need some professional advice. The man who took him is to call back and give me information on his return, but he told me not to contact the police so I don't want anyone to know that I have talked with you."

"Suppose I come to your home like I was a salesman or something," the man said, "and I can get all the information and check out the scene."

"Oh yes, please, come as soon as you can."

"Well, it is almost 11:00 p.m. now and it would seem strange to anyone watching your house for me to show up at this hour unless you are used to receiving gentlemen callers at night. Perhaps around 8:30 a.m. in the morning might be better," he said.

"Yes, of course, you are right. Everything must seem to be normal. Thank you for the suggestion. I will see you in the morning."

"What is your name and your husband's name and address and telephone number, in case I need to call before I come."

"Of course, how foolish of me, my name is Marissa Delclare and my husband's name is Jeffery Delclare, and we live at 782 Tamerlane Drive on the west side of town. Thank you, officer, for all the help."

"It is Detective, Mrs. Delclare, Detective Stephen McGuire, and it's no problem. I will see you tomorrow. Now you get some sleep and don't worry, we will find your husband." The line clicked as the man on the other end hung up.

Marissa hung the phone up and shook her head. Surely this was not the same Stephen that she had known. There had to be another person by the same name working at the sheriff's office. She would think about all this in the morning, but for now, she was exhausted. The mental fatigue was setting in and she could hardly hold her head up. She turned to Elaine and felt herself falling ever so slowly to the floor.

Elaine caught her as she fell and was able to move her to the loveseat in the library. Then she checked her pulse and she felt the strong beating of her heart. A faint, though frightening to those around them, was never of concern for the one who had fainted and so she covered Marissa with an afghan and pulled off her shoes. Knowing there was nothing else she could do for her, she set the alarm system at the door and let herself out. She would be back in the morning to see what the police were going to do about Jeff. And she needed to be fresh herself if she was going to be any help to Marissa.

Stephen hung up the phone and sat looking at it for a very long time. He had known her voice the moment she spoke. It was like free falling into the past. He had thought that he could talk to her and remain indifferent. Nope, indifferent was the last thing he felt right now. She sounded so vulnerable on the phone. He guessed she really loved this Delclare guy. Well, that wouldn't stop him from having his say. He had never really gotten over her rejection of him, he had loved her from the first moment he had seen her in the study hall all those years ago and, though he wasn't as good with words as she was, he thought she knew it.

When he had proposed to her that night so many years ago, he'd had to have a few drinks to screw up his courage. He wanted her and he didn't want her, he needed her and he had tried to stay away from her. She had him twisted in so many knots that he didn't know which way was up most of the time. All he knew was he loved her and that hadn't changed in the years since he had tried to put her out of his mind, even after his marriage to someone else. It was still buried down there in a smoldering heap. All those memories of his youth captured in his Marissa's eyes. Why hadn't he made her realize how important she was to him? Why couldn't he get the words out? Someday....

November 12, 2001, 8:00 a.m.

"Bzzzzz." The light filtered in through the library doors where the curtains were ajar and warmed her face, what was that buzzing sound? Were there bees in the house? Why was she so warm? Her mind slowly surfaced and she saw that she was lying on the library loveseat covered by an afghan. How had she gotten here? The last thing she remembered was talking to the man on the phone at the sheriff's department.

"Bzzzzz." What was that buzzing sound? She shook her head trying to clear her thoughts and immediately realized that it was the doorbell she was hearing. Of course, that was it, the doorbell. She crossed the library floor heading for the front door. Without thinking, she threw open the door, and immediately set off the burglar alarm. Oh my God! Trying to act as normal as possible she motioned to the man standing there that she would be right back and ran for the control panel to turn the thing off. When she returned, she found him still standing on the front porch, briefcase in hand, waiting for her to invite him in.

"Hello, I'm Steve McGuire and you called about wanting an estimate for our services. May I come in, Mrs. Delclare?" Detective McGuire inquired.

"Yes, please, please come in, forgive my appearance. It seems my friend must have put me to bed on the couch last night," Marissa stuttered. She felt a fool because, of course, it was the Stephen McGuire of her past and he was grinning widely at her confusion. She could have slapped him, this was a serious situation, but then she realized how inept the response she had made was and started to smile herself.

"I mean, my friend Elaine was here helping me and I was so exhausted after I talked with you that I just collapsed and I guess...." Her voice trailed off. Stephen stopped grinning and took in her appearance in a different light. Of course, she was exhausted; she was not used to having her husband kidnapped in the middle of the day and then come home and find her home ransacked to boot. The stress alone must have been horrendous. He was sorry that he had seemed to take her less than seriously. They had better get down to business. He looked at her intently and asked, "Marissa are you all right? I knew as soon as I heard your voice that it was you last night, but I didn't want to say anything until I had seen you in person just to make sure that I wasn't wrong."

"Oh, Stephen," she sobbed, "someone has taken Jeff, what am I going to do?" She felt him gather her in his arms and she wept uncontrollably while they stood in the middle of her front hall. Finally some minutes later, when it seemed that her eyes could not get any itchier and her head could not pound any harder, she sat down to tell Stephen the entire story. When she had finished, he looked around the room and began to take notes. Then he opened the briefcase and began to dust the entire house with white powder and take prints from all the obvious places. He asked her who had been in the house that day besides Jeff and herself.

"Only Elaine and the man who had done all this."

"Well," Stephen said, "have you found the book?"

"No," Marissa answered, "I didn't want to disturb anything before you got here and then there was the taped message from Jeff saying he had put them somewhere."

"Taped message," said Stephen, "what taped message?"

"It was on the answering machine along with the other messages of that day. Along with the message from the man who has taken him."

"Does your husband have any enemies who might be using this as a cover to get back at him?"

"Heavens no, everyone likes Jeff. I am surprised you should even suggest it."

"We have to look at all aspects of a case. Don't be upset, I didn't mean to imply that he was the sort who would make enemies. But sometimes there are people who take offense at the smallest things and even disgruntled employees act on their impulses. We have to be sure it isn't something like that," Stephen stated.

He crossed to the answering machine and began to listen to the messages just as Marissa had the day before. When he had finished, he popped the tape out of the machine and pocketed it. "I am going to take this to our lab and see if they can get anything else off of it," Stephen said. "Meanwhile, just start searching and I will have a wiretap set in motion for your phone. If the man calls again, keep him talking for as long as you can, get him to let you talk to Jeff. If he says he won't, tell him that you don't believe that Jeff is alive and if he isn't you will never give him the book. If he puts Jeff on, ask only yes or no questions, and see if you can ascertain where he put the books, explain that the tape ran out and you didn't get the location that he said."

"Okay, will you be here when he calls? I'm going to need all the moral support I can get."

"Can you call someone to be here with you? I will be, if I can, but I need to check out some things back at the office."

"Yes, I understand, Elaine will probably be coming by soon anyway, I will wait for her. Thanks for all your help, Stephen. I never expected to see you in my house in this way."

"Marissa, keep your chin up, you are a strong lady, you can handle this. I heard about your husband's accident and how his wife held up under all the strain, even though I didn't know she was you. If you can handle that, you can handle this. Just know that it will all come right in the end," Stephen said as he closed his briefcase. He took the camera that he had in his pocket and began snapping pictures of the crime scene and then when he had finished, he turned to give Marissa a thumbs-up signal and let himself out the door.

Marissa sat down on the edge of the loveseat with her head in her hands. Could she handle this? Could she really find a way out of this? Could Jeff survive the treatment that he was undoubtedly going through? Pray he could and would continue to hold on until she found a way to get to him. Pray Stephen would see some clue that she had overlooked. Pray they all would be kept safe.

CHAPTER ELEVEN

June 1847

The breezes blew off the ocean from the south now and carried with them the kiss of summer. All around Seacliff the plants and flowers that were a mere promise the year before struggled up and burst into riotous color. As Catherine took the morning walk that the physician had advised her was best for her health during her pregnancy, she wandered back and forth through the gardens and along the cliffside looking out to sea. It was June and the life growing within her had made itself felt only yesterday, the tiny fluttering of butterfly wings against her insides reminding her of the eyelash kisses Mamma had used to give her as a child. Oh, Mamma, how I wish you were here to be with me in the coming days, how happy you would be to have another child to rock and cuddle. How I miss you. Sweet woman of my infancy.

"Miss Cathy, Miss Cathy," the maid called. "Please come up to the house now, you have a visitor."

"I'm coming, right away, make them comfortable and I will be there shortly." Cathy quickened her pace and headed toward the house. The house from this angle by the sea had a brooding look, the balconies throwing shadows, like eyelids, over the windows and doors below. It showed its best face from the front toward the drive where the verandahs advertised welcome and peace.

Theresa waited in the hall. "Miss Caroline is come to see you, Miss Cathy."

Catherine hurried forward to greet her. They were almost the same distance in their pregnancy, Caroline only a month or so ahead of her. Caroline already looked much larger than Catherine and was ravenously hungry all the time. This child would surely be a large one and Catherine worried that the delivery would be difficult. That was still some months away, time to worry then.

"Caroline, how wonderful to see you. I hope all is well with Captain Smith and you," Catherine spoke first.

"Oh, quite wonderful, only I escaped to your gorgeous home to get away from the oppressive heat in the city today. Here it is only June and already the perspiration drips from me if I even lift a finger to do anything. I am prostrate from the heat most of the day. I came to enjoy your ocean precipice and let the breezes cool my brow!" Caroline exclaimed.

It was indeed cooler here, the windows of the house were thrown wide to catch the breeze from any direction and the curtains fluttered as it wiggled through and cooled them.

Caroline looked at Catherine, she looked wonderful, with the bloom of health that only young pregnant women had. She was at least eleven years older than the younger woman and her pregnancy weighed heavily on her, but the joy of at last producing a child swept it from her thoughts and she rejoiced to be here with her friend.

She took Catherine's arm and they strolled into the conservatory where the sky and sea could be observed while the breezes blew and they ordered cold drinks and refreshments.

"Catherine, I have news of Edgar. Captain Smith landed in Richmond to pick up some passengers who had booked from there to England, and he happened to see a copy of a newspaper with a column by Edgar. So there we have found him, what do you intend to do?" Caroline questioned.

"Why, I don't intend to do anything. I have already told you that Edgar must come on his own or not at all. Why do you ask?" Catherine stated.

"I only ask because there have been inquiries about you in the city," Caroline offered.

"Inquiries, what kind of inquiries?" she asked.

"It seems that there is a certain gentleman asking about you around the city, and, of course, so far your friends have refused to give any information," Caroline said.

"This gentleman, did he give his name?" Catherine wondered.

"I think that someone said he called himself, Daniel Graves," Caroline stated.

"Daniel! I have not heard that name since leaving England. I wonder if it could be the same as I had known at home," Catherine cried.

"Do you want me to make inquiries for him?" Caroline asked.

"Yes, please do find out if he is from England and where he knows me from. If he states that I lived in his house, then it is the one," Catherine exclaimed.

"You lived in his house?" Caroline inquired. "How is that, is he a relative then?"

"No, no, my mamma rented the house from his father, and he inherited the properties from him." Catherine laughed. It was good to hear her laugh again. Since Edgar had left there had not been much laughter. Caroline had worried at her isolation at Seacliff.

"Oh then, it is quite all right. I will send the servants to find the information on my return and if he is the same, I will send him to you. I feel that you need all the familiar faces that you can have right now." Caroline decided to do it that very week, just as soon as she could. Catherine was unhappy and she needed to be cheered. The handsome man that she had seen from afar, and who was pointed out to her as the one desiring to find Catherine Barrett, might be just the one to do it.

"Caroline, I am so glad you have come, you have given me something to look forward to and I have a gift for you too," Catherine said as she crossed to her desk and pulled open a drawer. Inside resided a number of small volumes. She pulled a copy out of the drawer and crossed back to Caroline. Handing it to her, she said, "I have written on the fly cover my feelings about our friendship, I hope you will enjoy them." The volume that Caroline was holding was inscribed and signed inside by the hand of Catherine. The signature was bold and clear. Catherine Barrett-Poe. The title on the side read *Timeless* while the author's name again was repeated on the spine, Catherine Aurora Barrett-Poe.

Caroline looked at Catherine and exclaimed, "Catherine, are you and Edgar truly married then?"

"No, not by the courts or church, but I am married to him by the only thing that matters, in the sight of God, and, I will be his or no one's in this life." Catherine sighed. Caroline wondered if that might change after Daniel arrived, but she said nothing.

The two women began to compare notes on their respective pregnancies and spent the week happily reveling in each other's company.

November 12, 2001, 10:00 a.m.

Marissa had just finished picking up all the papers and debris that had been scattered around when the doorbell began buzzing again. She crossed the hall and opened the door. It was Elaine, come to see how she was doing.

"Can I help you today, pick up, fix you something to eat, you look like a train wreck. Why don't you go upstairs and take a shower? I will listen for the phone," Elaine said.

"I will take a bath but I will have the carry-around phone with me, I have some specific things that I am supposed to ask the kidnapper and I don't want to forget anything," Marissa answered.

"What things, how do you know what to say?" asked Elaine.

"The detective was here this morning from the sheriff's office and we went over how I should handle any phone calls," she said.

"Good," Elaine replied, "is the detective coming back here?"

"Not right away," Marissa said, "he needs to check into some things at the office and he took a lot of pictures and dusted for prints. He will be back as soon as he gets things set up for the phone calls."

"Okay, get a bath and freshen up. I will fix you some breakfast, you need to eat, stress will kill you if you don't stay on top of your game. So go on now and it will be ready when you get done," Elaine finished as she walked into the kitchen.

Marissa slowly climbed the stairs as though she were a very old woman, which she wasn't, but which she felt like at the moment. Where was the excitement that she had had on entering the house yesterday? She was going to have to have nerves of steel to get through this. She wished her mother were here to lean on and talk with, but her mom had gone to her reward five years before followed shortly by her dad so there was no one to unburden herself to. Her brother, Ryan, had died suddenly the year before and her younger brother, Richard, was flying all over the country for his company. She doubted that she could even get a hold of him. How had her life become so encapsulated? Jeffery had become her whole life. She couldn't even call the girls and let them know what had happened to their father. She knew Sandy and Willow would be upset when they found that she hadn't told them right away, but she just couldn't take the chance. She was too afraid that they might jeopardize the situation by something they might say to friends. Leslie was still in North Dakota and too far to divulge a secret but she couldn't tell one child without telling the others, so she too must be kept in the dark. Leon was incommunicado underwater for the Navy. So for right now it was just she and Elaine and Stephen and any others at the sheriff's department who might have an interest in the crime.

She walked into the bedroom and began to strip off her clothes, piece by piece, while she turned on the hot water and watched the tub filling. When she was really tired and worn down, a hot tub of bubbles was the only way to unwind. Often when Jeff was waiting for her in bed to finish her nightly soak, she would slip off to sleep in the hot water relaxing completely. It was a wonder that she hadn't drowned before this. Only now there was no Jeff waiting for her under the covers. Just the empty room and the empty bed. After all the nights while Jeff recovered, she had just gotten used to having him beside her in the night again. When would she have him there once more?

She stepped into the hot water and let the warmth seep into her tired and cramped muscles. She hadn't gotten the proper rest on the loveseat last night, though it had been better than no rest at all. Now she could really feel the water doing its trick and she could see Jeff's form behind her eyelids. She could see him speaking to her but couldn't quite make out the words. What was he trying to tell her? Something about the book, something about a poem, it's almost here, I almost have it. She drifted off in a drowsy nap.

"Marissa, Marissa," yelled Elaine, "are you all right? I am putting breakfast on the table. Come on down and eat this while it is hot."

"Oh! Oh, okay," called Marissa, "I'll be right down." Marissa sat up in the hot water and blinked the sleep out of her eyes. She had fallen asleep. She shouldn't let herself do that. She started to dry off and remembered…. There was something in her mind that she had to write down, right now before she forgot it. Now where was a pad and pencil? Oh, there was one on the nightstand by the bed. She grabbed the pencil and began writing. Why was this so important? She finished the poem, because that's what it was, she recognized, as soon as she started writing. Why was she writing poetry now? What was the significance of the poem? She threw on her robe, grabbed the pad, and hurried downstairs to see what culinary magic Elaine had been working in the kitchen.

The table was set with plates and cups and saucers and the coffee smelled delicious. There were bowls of scrambled eggs and rashers of bacon, and stacks of toast with jelly and butter. It looked as though she was expecting to feed a crowd, but Marissa forgot the amounts as she began to eat. She realized that this was the first food she had had since lunch the day before. After she had washed down the food with her first cup of coffee, she grabbed another and picked up the pad that she had been writing on.

"What do you have there?" asked Elaine.

"Well, you are going to think I am nuts, but while I was in the bath, I dozed off and during the nap I could have sworn that Jeff came and was saying these things to me. When I woke to hear you calling, I wrote down what I could remember him saying, and this is what I remember," Marissa replied.

"Read it to me," Elaine said. She knew that Marissa and Jeff were on pretty much the same mental wavelength, so she didn't poo poo what Marissa had said out of hat.

"Okay," Marissa said, "here goes.

> "'It is always darkest before the dawn.'
> Someone said that a long time ago
> Who it was somehow I don't remember right now
> Or maybe I never did know.
>
> It's true enough though in the wee tiny hour
> Just before the first light shows through
> There's nary a trace of tree, house, or flower
> Can be seen in the fresh rising dew.
>
> How is it that in the time before light
> We can feel their presence so near?
> The loved ones we knew, their forms pure and bright,
> And behold them without any fear.
>
> Are they just there behind the lids
> Of our eyes fast closed in our sleep?
> Promising never to leave us behind
> Remembering the vows that they keep.
>
> Are they the angels we heard of when young
> That mothers would speak of to child?
> Are they those mothers themselves who are sung
> Of in ballads so meek and so mild?
>
> No matter what, it's a comfort to know
> There is something or someone waiting for me
> When I close my eyes and my breath slows
> And my soul starts its traveled road free.

"That is it," Marissa said, "that is the whole thing."

"You mean, you wrote that after I called you to come to breakfast and before you came down," Elaine said.

"Yes," Marissa replied, "it is exactly as I remember hearing him say in my dream."

"Unbelievable!" exclaimed Elaine. "Do you think it is from the book you are looking for, maybe? Perhaps to help you convince the caller when he calls that you have the book after all!"

"I never thought of that, but perhaps you are right. The only thing I can do is try it and see, since I haven't got the book and only the person who had the book originally would know," Marissa replied.

"Do you remember the place where you bought the box of books that this book was in? Maybe the police can check with them and see if they know anything about where the book came from in the first place," Elaine suggested.

"Yes, I remember the place but it was an auction and I am sure that the people who ran it were just agents, but perhaps they could supply the heir's names. This was an estate auction after all," Marissa mused. "I will call the detective soon and give him this information."

"Will you be all right if I run some errands and pick up some things for your refrigerator? I kind of depleted it this morning with all this and you will need something for the rest of the week, especially if you are going to hug the phone," Elaine said.

"Sure, I will be fine. Do you have a key to the back door? Here, use Jeff's, then you won't have to stand outside and buzz yourself in," Marissa suggested.

Elaine shouldered on her jacket and grabbed her purse. She smiled at Marissa and hurried out the door. She was shaking her head as she got into the car, she thought that perhaps Marissa was grabbing at straws with this poem.

Marissa began to look through her checkbook for the name of the auctioneer or the people who had held the sale where she had bought the box of books. It had to be in the last few months, because Jeff had been in the hospital for weeks and she had gone to the auction right before the accident. Oh, there it was, September 22, 2001. A check in the amount of $15.00 made out to the estate of Meredith Joan Montgomery Warren. Perhaps this would help the police, and if she could get a hold of the genealogy books at the library she would look up the person of the estate. Maybe that might throw some light on the whole story.

Meanwhile back to the mystery of what Jeff could have done with the books. She had looked the house over and found no sign of them which meant Jeff had discovered something about the books and had decided to do a little digging of his own. Who would he have called or mentioned it to? Donna, his secretary at work? Some of the researchers on the staff at the publishing company? Or some of his cronies in the publishing business? Had he contacted the Library of Congress as she had? Too many questions and not enough answers. She was having a hard time being patient and waiting for the phone to ring. She took the new poem, the one that Jeff had given her in her sleep, and went into the library. Seated at the desk, it was as if none of this was really happening. Jeff would come down pretty soon from upstairs and they would laugh at the silliness of the dream that she had had about all this. Surely, this was just a bad dream; a nightmare and she would soon wake. Surely, this wasn't really happening to her.

"Riinnnngg." She started in her seat and stared at the phone on the desk. "Riinngggg," it went again. She grabbed for the receiver and slowly brought it to her ear, dreading the sound of the voice, which would make the nightmare even more real.

"Marissa, this is Stephen." Oh, thank God, it wasn't the man, it was Stephen and he would tell her that he had information and they were going at this minute to find Jeff.

"Marissa, are you there?"

"Yes, Stephen, I'm here, what is the news? Do you know anything yet? Have you found Jeff?"

"There is no news yet, Marissa, but I do have the telephone tap set up and we will be monitoring all the phone calls in and out of your house now. The fingerprint files are not all run yet and the voice matching of the tape is still to be finished. These things take time, you know. You will have to be patient."

"I'm sorry, I guess I am just expecting this to be a bad dream and when more things keep cropping up I don't know what to think."

"What things? What do you mean more things? Has he called back yet? We don't have any record of it, but I guess he could have called you before we got the phones bugged."

"No, he hasn't called but my friend, Elaine, was here with me fixing breakfast and while she was in the kitchen, I went up to take a soaking bath. I was trying to get rid of some of this tension and while I was in the tub, I had a vision of Jeff and he was trying to tell me something. When I woke up I had a poem in my head and I immediately wrote it down. It was a poem he seemed to be reciting to me. Like maybe he wanted me to use it to fool the kidnapper into thinking I had the books. I don't know but that's all I can think of," she said. "Also, I found the name of the person who I bought the box of books from. It was the estate of Meredith Joan Montgomery Warren. I have the check dated September 22, 2001, in my canceled checks. I thought you might be able to find out something about the man from the people who ran the sale or maybe the family would know something."

"Good idea, I will get right on it. And that thing about the poem, can't hurt to try, he maybe won't know all the poems in the book, but if he does, then you can stall for time and tell him that the poem was in another book that your husband had," he said. "I will come out later today and see how you are doing and take a look at the poem that Jeff gave you."

"You don't think I am crazy for thinking Jeff gave it to me in a dream."

"Listen, kiddo, you have always been pretty close to the spirit world, I would believe anything you tell me. You always had my number pretty good in the past. But maybe now is not the time to talk about that," he said. "Take care and I'll see you later."

He hung up the phone and sat looking at it for a long time. No, now was not the time to talk to Marissa about the past. She had too much on her plate for that but some day he would tell her the truth about his feelings for her. He didn't want to give her anything else to focus on now, but ever since that night so many years ago when he had asked her to marry him, she had been in the back of his mind.

Yes, he had been angry and hurt, he had vowed never to speak to her again, but the feelings he had for her were too strong and he had tried to find her after his first year in college only to find that she had married someone else. Some Feinstein character. He had done some checking but the guy didn't have a record, just didn't have a very good track record with women. But she had married someone else and he would just get on with his life, and he had.

He had found a wonderful woman and married her, but she had not outlived him and he was alone again. He had sent a letter to her job hoping that she was free again. Hoping that this time he could convince her that he truly loved her, and now she had married someone else for a second time. This time, though, the guy really loved her and it looked as though the feelings were returned. He would have to wait and see how everything turned out. He had waited this long, he could wait longer. He loved her, always had and always would, even though he probably would never have the dream he dreamed of.

He could still feel the touch of her lips on his and the heady trembling of their youth when they had held each other so tightly, like neither one of them would ever let the other go. Why had they? What had he done to her that she had walked away? He knew that the night she had said he took her for granted, he knew he had, but she had always acted as though she wanted him to. Women, he would never figure them out.

July 1847

He didn't know what he expected, but certainly not this beautiful woman who crossed the hall floor to greet him. Catherine was radiant, her black curly hair billowing loose about her shoulders and her skin clear and unblemished. She was smiling at him as she took his hand in hers.

"Daniel, I am so happy to see you here. I thought never to see you again. What brings you to the States?" she said.

"I came to find you, Catherine," he replied. "And to perhaps see if this was indeed a place where a man could make his fortune. Are the streets here truly paved with gold as everyone at home seems to think?"

"There are riches to be made here," she replied, "but it is better if you start with money first."

"Then it is no different than at home, though there you need ancestry as well. Catherine, I see you have been busy since we were last together, this is a fine house and now I understand there will be a child. Where is the lucky father? When may I meet him? I waited for you long in England and then when no word came, I questioned my coachman and started on my search for you. I would have been here sooner, but my mother became ill and I was restrained from leaving England before now."

"Oh, I am sorry to hear of your mother's illness, I hope she is recovered now."

"Her illness was mortal and she is gone now to her reward. So back to the question of your lucky husband, when may I be introduced?"

"Daniel, you must not ask me of him, I cannot produce him at the present time, I must wait on him to come to me. Enough of the questions about me, let me look at you. How wonderful it is to see someone from home, though I should expect this is my home now. Would you like to see the grounds and house?"

"To be sure, I would like a tour, are you up to a stroll? I would not like to tire you unduly."

"Don't be silly, I am supposed to take the air and exercise daily. It is good for myself and the baby. Come now and see what I have created here on Long Island."

The views were reminiscent of the cliffs of Dover at home and he could understand why she had come to plant her house in this place. He himself could be quite comfortable here, and gardens and all around were immaculate. She must have good servants to keep this kind of home and gardens like this. As they strolled, he looked back on the house in the afternoon sun and it glowed with a golden hue as if sprinkled with golden dust and lit by firelight. He could see that she was satisfied here. Where was this elusive father and husband? Why was he absent from this gorgeous creature? If it were he, he would not be driven from her side. He had tarried too long in England and had lost his chance with her. No matter that duty prevented him, somehow he should have found a way.

"Will you be here long in the United States?" Catherine asked him.

"As long as need be to find an answer to the questions that I have."

"I see, then you will come and be my guest whenever the fancy strikes you, I insist."

"Then that will be the whole of the time I spend here. You will become tired of me I dare say, before I become bored with your company."

She had the grace to look at the ground, she knew him to be kindness personified. She needed to talk to someone about the future. Perhaps later on she could prevail on him to do her a courtesy, but for now they would enjoy each other's company.

November 2001

Stephen hung up the phone on his office desk and folded his hands in front of him. That last call was the key. He had talked with first one of the children of the deceased and than another, finally almost despairing of getting the information he needed, he had dailed the last child's number.

"Hello," came the feminine voice from the receiver.

"Hello, miss, I am sorry to bother you, but your brother and sisters told me that you may be able to help me with my investigation," Stephen started.

"What investigation?" the voice asked.

"Well, my name is Stephen McGuire and I'm a detective working on a kidnapping case involving a local publishing vice president, and his wife has a book that she bought at an auction recently, which I think your family owned."

"A book of poetry?"

"Why, yes, that's exactly what I am trying to find some facts about," he replied.

"What did you need to know about it?" the girl asked cautiously.

"Well, just who wrote it and why anyone would want to kidnap someone to get it?"

"I don't know much about the book myself, except that my mother told me that one day when I was old enough, she was going to give it to me for safekeeping. She seemed to think that it was important that it stay in our family."

"Why not give it to one of the others then?"

"Well, my sisters and brother are not really a part of my mother's family, being as they are my stepsisters and stepbrother, and I guess mother felt that I should have it since it really was all about one of my ancestors."

"And what else did she tell you?" Stephen pressed for all the information he could get.

"Well, she did say recently that someone had contacted her to try and buy the book, but that she had told her that it was not for sale, it was a family heirloom. That is all I know, except when I got back home from a trip after she had died, I found that the house had already been sold and everything in it disposed of. It was no one's fault that the book was put up for sale, just a mishap. My mother hadn't said anything about it to anyone but me, so when Penny and Denise had the sale, they naturally just sold it along with everything else."

"What happened to your mother? Did she die of natural causes?"

"Yes, as far as I know. Why, do you think someone would have harmed her to get the book?"

"Probably not, just an unhappy coincidence, but unfortunate that you missed keeping the book."

"Is there anything else I can help you with?" the girl answered.

"No, you have been a lot of help. By the way, what was your mother's maiden name?" Stephen asked.

"Montgomery, why do you ask?"

"Just curious, and do you know your grandfather and grandmother's name on your mother's side?" he asked pursuing the matter as far as it would go.

"Yes, it was Peter Edgar Montgomery and Sarah Joan Meredith. That's why my mother's name was Meredith."

"Well, thanks, miss, for all your help," Stephen answered.

"Sir, if you are able to, can you give me the name of the people who have my mother's book?" she asked.

"I can't give out that information now in the middle of an investigation, but I will get in touch if it becomes available later," Stephen finished and hung the phone on the cradle.

Ruth hung up the phone on her end of the line and sat down with her head in her hands.

CHAPTER TWELVE

1:00 p.m., Same Day

Marissa began looking through the books that were scattered around. They wouldn't be there, the kidnapper had already looked at them. She started stacking them in piles. What did he mean talk about the past? There was no past. She had given him an answer years ago and he had taken her at her word. There was no past. There was no future. She was Jeff's and would always be Jeff's. Surely there wasn't anything to talk about now. She wasn't sure that she knew what to say to him when he returned later. She would just put on her professional face and keep her distance from him. Stephen had a job to do and they were both adults.

There were still many books to go through on the shelves, her filing system was slightly out of date. Having a publisher for a husband meant that every time a new release came out of his shop, he would bring it home for her to read. She loved to read and there were many books on the shelf that she had not had time to look at. She kept telling herself that one of these days, one of these days, she would take time off and just read until she had had enough. But there was always this chore and that meeting and helping at the church and working in the volunteer organizations. It seemed that Jeff wanted her to fill her days and nights with things, so that when he had to be gone she would not miss him. Now she could not leave the house! She must stay and man the phones. So she would read and the time would pass. She had to stay awake so she would sit in a chair, not a really comfortable chair, so that she would not nod off as she was wont to do when she read in the evenings. She could stay awake because it was broad daylight now and there was no danger of her napping in the daytime. She had never been a nap taker.

She picked up the next book on the pile and looked at the jacket cover. There on the cover was the picture of a young girl staring back at her. A girl with haunting green eyes and wispy brown hair. The title of the book sounded familiar. *Because I Love You.* She opened the book and found that here indeed was another book of poetry, but the poems were so familiar. She looked again at the spine of the book jacket for the author's name. "Marissa Suellen Delclare." What is this? Where did this book come from? It wasn't here before. Was this something Jeff had sent over with the poetry book? Was this a surprise from him? What a surprise! No wonder she loved him to desperation. He was the most wonderful lover and husband. What would she do without him? "Oh, Jeff, I can't stand this." She started to weep, silently and steadily until great sobs were welling up inside her and streams of tears poured down her cheeks. "What will I do without him?"

She held the little volume close to her heart and began to think of the writer of the other book, Catherine Aurora Barrett-Poe. Why had she never heard of the name of Poe in connection with another poet? She had, of course, read all of Edgar Allen's works many times, but the poems in Catherine's volume had been different entirely. They were happy for the most part and full of hope and confident of the future. Some leaned towardand looked longingly into the future. She hadn't had time to read all the works but the ones that she remembered were filled with promise and love and caring. She had a set of encyclopedias on the shelf, why not look up the families of both Poe and Barrett and see what the encyclopedia had to say about them. That was better than sitting on her hands and doing nothing. Besides, she doubted that she could read anything else right now anyway. She had never been a do-nothing kind of person and she wasn't about to start now.

She crossed to the shelves and pulled the volume lettered B and began to look up the information on the Barretts. Elizabeth was, after all, a famous English poet of her time. Let's see, what is this here? She saw there that Elizabeth wasn't married until 1846. Perhaps she had had a dalliance or even was abused and raped and couldn't or wouldn't divulge the name of the father. Perhaps there was a child, one who would embarrass the family. Perhaps Catherine had been put out to be cared for under Elizabeth's family name. Maybe a furious father would force her to cut all ties with the child in order for him to settle funds on it and see to its upbringing. That would explain Elizabeth's ill health for so long and her seclusion that was common knowledge of the day. If that was the case, it was entirely possible that the money would be available to Catherine to immigrate to the United States when she became old enough to travel on her own. Marissa could believe a father could be so unfeeling; after all, hadn't hers been out of her life pretty much all the time also? Why not believe a grandfather would not want the disgrace as well.

137

"I'll bet that is what happened, I'll bet Catherine came to this country and met Edgar at a social gathering of writers and became infatuated him." Looking in the volume under P, she found that Edgar was married to his cousin Virginia during this period. She wondered why Catherine might have been attracted to him. "But wait, it said that Virginia died in 1847 so Edgar would have been free also. Perhaps they were caught up with each other, swept away by feelings to strong to deny and the poems that she wrote were for him. She must have been a great writer of poetry herself, for her to complete all the poetry I saw in that small volume," she whispered to herself. So many questions, she wondered, were there really any answers?

August 1847

Daniel came through the conservatory door to find Catherine seated at her desk writing a document. He had entered so silently that she was unaware of his presence and he stood watching her as she carefully folded the paper that she had been working on and slipped it back into the drawer. He cleared his throat, and she turned, startled at his figure standing there. He was a fine figure of a man and she truly was fond of him. He had been here in her house now for over a month and never a comment on where was the absent father. She didn't deserve a friend such as him and she knew that it was hard for him to see her pregnant with another man's child. If she had stayed in England, might he have courted her in truth? But that was a "what if" and she had long ago stopped asking them in her heart. That way only led to sadness and depression, it would not do to dwell in that frame of mind now. She must keep her spirits high for the sake of the child; too much sadness might mark the child and that she'd never allow to happen if she could prevent it.

"Am I disturbing you? I noticed you were writing. I can take a walk around the grounds and come back later if you like," Daniel asked.

"Not at all, it was just a note for the maid and I can see to it later. Come let us both go for a walk, for I have sat at this desk long enough now and I need to stretch my legs. Wait while I get a parasol, the weather may turn threatening before we return."

The summer squalls were brief there on the island, but, even with the warm sun, could produce a drenching in a short minute or two. It wouldn't do to get a soaking. It was August now and soon the days would begin to shorten. The birth lay only four months away. She now must leave the stays off and allow the child room to grow. And though her figure was filling, Daniel did not find her unattractive, as he saw only the glow that emanated from her face and eyes. She was so beautiful, sometimes to look at her took his breath away.

"Come, take my arm and we shall walk to the cliff and back and see if the seagulls are flying about," he said.

"Yes, it's coolest there by the shore, perhaps we can take the path to the beach. Sometimes the dolphins play in the shallows among the rocks, that is a sight you haven't seen yet," Catherine replied.

"Can you make the climb back up?" he asked. "I don't want you to tire yourself unnecessarily. I can see the dolphins another time or after the birth, if I am still here for that."

"Would you stay that long, then?" she whispered.

"As long as that and longer if you desire."

"You are too good to me. I have come to depend on you so much. Are you sure you wouldn't be happier out of my presence, since I have grown so large?"

"No, but if you tire of me, then by all means, send me away, I would not presume to bore you longer than you want."

"I am not bored with you, but I might put you to work for me." She laughed.

"Anything, just name it."

The moment of seriousness was broken, but the thoughts lay there in each mind. Perhaps there was a chance, he thought. And perhaps here is one who will help me, she thought.

"I have thought to bring Caroline here for the rest of this hot weather, while she can still travel, though soon it will be too late, and I was wondering if you could fetch her for me. I think that Captain Smith's ship is still another month at sea. I think she would enjoy both of our companies and I long to set my thoughts at rest about her. She is not due to have the baby until the end of October."

"Your wish is my command, I will leave on tomorrow's early ferry and fetch her here before supper, or my name's not Daniel Bartholomew Graves."

"Bartholomew," she said laughing.

"Don't laugh, my mother wanted a distinguished sounding name and so it is."

"All right then, I will expect you both tomorrow evening."

November 12, 2001, 2:45 p.m.

Just as the door opened, the phone started ringing. Marissa ran to answer it.

"Hello," she spoke into the receiver, "this is Marissa."

"Yes, did you find the book? Your husband is not doing too well, so if you have found it, I suggest you tell me," the unidentified voice demanded.

"Yes, I found it, just tell me where to go and I will bring it to you." Elaine was standing now, listening at the corner of the doorway to the kitchen.

"How do I know you have the book? Read me something out of it!"

"Just a minute while I get it," she answered, she frantically searched the top of the desk for the pad she had written the poem from Jeff on.

"All right, here it is, but be warned that I insist on talking to my husband first before I take it anywhere. So let's get that straight right now."

"He is all right and you will see him as soon as you give me the book," the man growled.

"That is not good enough, no Jeff on the phone, no book. I will not be satisfied he is all right until I hear his voice."

"All right, I will call you back and you can talk with him, now let's hear that poem."

She cleared her throat and began to read,

> "'It is always darkest before the dawn.'
> Someone said that a long time ago.
> Who it was somehow I don't remember right now
> Or maybe I never did know.
>
> It's true enough though in the wee tiny hour
> Just before the first light shows through
> There's nary a trace of tree, house, or flower
> Can be seen in the fresh rising dew.
>
> How is it that in the time before light
> We can feel the presence so near?
> The loved ones we knew, their forms pure and bright
> And behold them without any fear.

Are they just there behind the lids
Of our eyes fast closed in our sleep?"

"That's enough, it's called 'Inside My Eyes.' I guess you do have the book. I will be back in touch with you, Mrs. Delclare." The man hung up and Marissa sank into the chair, wilted like a flower left too long away from water and sun.

Elaine rushed to her side and hugged her. "You did great, I hope that the police have gotten the trace on that call."

"So do I, because I don't have a clue yet where the books are."

"I thought you told him you had found them," Elaine said.

"I had to play along with him and I also have an idea that might fool him, if I can't find them in time." She wondered why the man had accepted the poem she had read so quickly.

"What is your idea?" Elaine asked.

"Sit and listen, you'll understand." Marissa picked up the phone again and called the publishing company.

"Donna," Marissa began, "do you remember the book that my husband had published for me as a surprise?"

"Sure, how do you like it?"

"I love it, but do you have a couple extra copies? I need for you to make two more copies, but put them in green leather covers and change the title to read *Timeless*. Put the author's name on the spine only in gold foil and show it to be Catherine Aurora Barrett-Poe. But just the title on the front."

"What's going on, Marissa? Why do you want to change the author's name and the title of your book?" Donna asked.

"Donna, this is a matter of life and death, and I can't explain right now, but I need those two books yesterday. So, for all of our sakes, put a rush on it and have them hand carried to me ASAP."

"Okay, I will stop the men and get someone on rebinding two copies right away. Is two copies enough?"

"Yes, that'll do the job, I hope. Thanks, Donna, and I'll explain one day but I just can't right now."

Elaine looked at her in wonder, what book was she talking about now? Marissa crossed to the library table and handed her a small book. She looked at the spine and saw Marissa's name on the book. What was this? She opened it and began to read the poetry that was finely typed and filled page after page. She knew that Marissa liked to write but hadn't realized that she had created enough for a book.

"You are going to try to pass your book off as hers. I hope it works, otherwise Jeff could be in big trouble."

"I know, but I have to have books of poetry and when I was looking at the book that Jeff had had done for me, the idea came to me. Perhaps the kidnapper is not too familiar with the poetry or has never actually read the book he is after. Maybe he is working for someone else. If that is the case, it might just work. Even if it doesn't at least the police will be watching me deliver them and can maybe catch whoever comes to collect them."

Elaine shrugged. "I hope you are right because if you aren't, I don't think there will be enough left of you to pick up the pieces if anything happens to Jeff."

She left the room and went to the kitchen to put away the groceries and things she had brought.

Marissa went to her room to rest. The mental games that she had been forced to play exhausted her, and she couldn't think straight. Maybe she had been wrong to tell the man she had the book. She needed to talk with Jeff. She needed to tell him she had not found the books yet and where had he put them? She needed to tell him about the lie she was trying to bring off. She just needed to hear his voice and know that he was still okay. She drifted off to sleep, tossing and turning with anxiety.

CHAPTER THIRTEEN

September 1847

Daniel arrived at Caroline's home mid-morning and knocked sharply at the door. The maid let him into the hallway and went to fetch her mistress. Daniel looked at the house with a critical eye, comfortable but not ostentatious, definitely a better neighborhood. Perhaps there were other properties available here to buy. He hadn't decided if he would invest in this country or not, but the vistas that he had seen so far were intriguing. He was not rich, but had a comfortable living afforded by the properties in England. Were he to sell and buy here, he doubted that he could afford anything as grand as Seacliff. Perhaps here in New York City, itself, there would be better chance to extend his fortune and his holdings.

There was Caroline coming toward him. She did not look as well as Catherine did, but of course she was some years older and this first pregnancy was telling on her. She had a smile on her face, nonetheless, and held her hands out in greeting.

"Mr. Graves, what a nice surprise! There is nothing wrong with Catherine, is there? I hadn't heard from either of you in such a long time. I confess that I was beginning to fret some in suspense. Now that you are here and you do not seem agitated, my mind is set at rest. What can I do for you on this visit?"

"Please, call me Daniel, Mr. Graves was always my father, and we are not so far apart in age that you need treat me as an elder."

"Well, then Daniel it is, and to what do I owe the honor of this visit?"

"I am come on a errand of mercy. Catherine perishes from too much of my company and wishes me to fetch you to the breezes and comfort of Seacliff."

"Oh, what a lovely idea, though I think the first part is an exaggeration. I was just thinking the other day, how much I missed visiting with her and wished for a way to do so, but with Captain Smith still at sea, I dare not strike out on my own at this juncture of my waiting. But now with you here, I will surely go. Will you take refreshments while I gather the things I will need for the stay? How long does she want me for?"

"She knows you can't stay as long as you'd like but perhaps a month might be as long as you can remain away from home."

"Then a month it will be and I shall welcome it. Do sit yourself down and take tea while I get ready."

About an hour and half later, and with a servant to carry the heaviest trunks to the coach, they departed for the ferry. The crossing took but a short time and they were on the other side and already the change in the air started to benefit Caroline. The flushed cheeks and the swollen eyes began to subside and she was breathing much easier. Daniel could see that indeed Catherine had been wise in surmising that Caroline would need to be out of the city at this time. She was wise in many things it seemed.

There in the evening sunset, glistening like spun gold at the end of the long drive, was Seacliff to welcome them both home, with Catherine standing on the verandah with her hand to shade her eyes watching for them.

The two women threw themselves on each other's shoulders in welcome, with tears of joy glistening in their eyes, and Daniel standing a little away compared the two, the older, and more heavily laden, one with the younger, not yet so swollen, one. They were a foil for each other, the one with dark hair wildly curling and quicksilver eyes, and the other fair and blue eyed with tendrils of blonde curls around the face like wisps of feathers to frame it. He was happy to have done this thing for them both. It would be good for each to compare the changes in their bodies and see if anything might be amiss. He was no good for that.

They went into the dining room where a light supper was laid, with cool soups and light fish dishes and fruits of every type arrayed.

"I thought you might need refreshment after the coach rides and ferry trip. If you don't find what you like here, just say the word, and I will try to get it for you," Catherine said.

"Everything looks delicious, Cathy, and I am sure that Daniel is hungry after the trip. I, myself, would like only a little fish and cold soup. I find that too many fruits are unpleasant for me now, and I have had my share at breakfast. Though you must eat yourself, as I see you have waited for us."

They sat down and took their choices and the meal passed fairly quietly. Daniel did not join the conversation of the two women, and sensing that they would like privacy, he feigned the need for a pipe and a walk along the shore and left them to themselves.

"Cathy, I can see that Daniel is indeed in love with you. Would you not at least consider him, if Edgar does not return?" Caroline asked at length when her soup and plate had been cleared.

"He is kindness in itself, but I have an obligation to remain for Edgar, it is his son that I bear. It is he that I have given my heart and body to."

"And if it is not returned, what then, my dear, what then?"

"I will cross that bridge when I come to it. Now enough of me and my life, what of you, how are you feeling? Is everything all right with you?"

"I confess I was very uncomfortable until I got to the Island and to Seacliff, but I feel right as rain now. This place should be made available to all sick people; they would be immediately made well. There is something in the air here."

"Caroline, I have a very big favor to ask of you. I don't want you to answer right away. I want to you to think about it before you answer."

"All right, what is it?"

"If something should happen to me during the birth of my child or after, would you take it and raise it as your own? I mean if Edgar does not come and claim it. I am drawing up a will that all my property, this house, my bank accounts are to be made over to my child on my death, with you and Captain Smith as guardians in Edgar's absence. I would like you to come and live here with your family. I have thought this out very carefully and I know this is the right thing to do."

"And what of Daniel, what of him? Does he not enter into any of this?"

"If I die in childbirth, he must have a free life of his own and not be burdened with a child from another man. If I survive, then this is all moot. The future will unroll as it will. But if I do die, I want to make sure that all is taken care of. Now think on this and consult with Captain Smith before answering. Let us speak no more of this and talk of other things now."

"All right, I will think on it," Caroline agreed but knew already in her heart that she would love Catherine's unborn child as much as her own and would have no trouble with the conditions of her request.

The House on Tamerlane
November 12, 2001, 4:00 p.m.

Several hours later, the doorbell buzzed and there on the porch stood a salesman with a briefcase in his hand. Elaine, inquiring if she could help him, was surprised to see a familiar face staring at her. The man was an older version of an old high school classmate. She remembered Stephen with black curly hair and warm brown eyes, but the man standing before her now was completely white-headed, though the eyes were still warm and brown.

"Stephen! You are the last person I expected to see when I opened this door. What on earth are you doing here?" Elaine exclaimed.

"Hello, Elaine, can I come in and explain. Where is Marissa?"

Elaine stood aside to let Stephen enter and then watched as he pulled out his shield which identified him as a detective with the sheriff's major case department. She looked at it and then at him.

"I didn't realize that you had gone into law enforcement after high school."

"After college, I still didn't know what I wanted to do, but since the Irish all become cops, I guess, I figured that was what I was best suited for," Stephen explained. "Is Marissa here?"

"Yes, of course, but she has been upstairs resting for the past couple of hours. Stay here and I'll go get her."

Elaine started up the stairs and met Marissa coming out of her room.

"I thought I heard voices down here."

"Stephen is here. You didn't tell me Stephen was the detective you talked with!"

"I guess with all the other things on my mind, it didn't seem that important."

They both moved down the stairs entering the library to find Stephen sitting in a chair looking at the book of poetry that Jeff had had published for her.

"I didn't know you wrote poetry," Stephen said.

"Yes, some for Jeff, and for the kids, and then sometimes just when the mood hits me."

"This looks pretty good to me," Stephen said. "I listened to the conversation you had with our chap on the phone. It might just work, this idea of yours about phony books disguised to look like the ones he wants."

"I know it's risky but until I find the real ones, it is all I can think of that might work."

"Well, there have been developments in the information you gave me. I took the names and dates you gave me and here is what we found. We questioned the children of Meredith Montgomery Warren and the only one who knew anything about the book was the youngest girl, Ruth. Her mother had told her years ago that the book was a family heirloom and was written by one of her ancestors. She wanted Ruth to have it when she was old enough, but time had slipped by and she had not thought of it again until recently when her mother mentioned that she had had inquiries about it. But then her mother had died and immediately after the funeral she had been called away to Europe on business and had failed to say anything about the book to her stepsisters or stepbrother. That was the reason you were able to get it at auction.

"When we knew that the book was a family heirloom it was an easy matter for our experts to check the data banks and trace the history back. Catherine Aurora Barrett was born in 1825 to Elizabeth Barrett, and, as you surmised, her father forced her to give up her infant. She was to have no further contact with her on the guarantee that the child would be raised in a good home. There was a further stipulation that upon coming into her adulthood, she would have an amount settle on her to enable her to live comfortably. She immigrated to the United States in 1843. We don't know whether she had letters of introduction to the social circle of writers of that time or if her talent opened doors for her here. In any case, we know she took Poe's name, whether or not she really married him, and was delivered of an infant son three years after arriving in the United States. He was born just before the year was over; no one knows what happened to the mother and infant son. Edgar may or may not have known about him. I like to think that he did not, for if he had, he may have had more reason for living.

"But whatever the case, Edgar was to die the next year at the age of forty. Whether Elizabeth and Robert ever knew that they had a grandson alive in the United States is a mystery, and whether they knew of Elizabeth's daughter's gift of the poetic form remains beyond our ken. But Jonathan Lee Poe survived, and continued the family heritage on through the years, finally arriving in our time in the person of Meredith Joan Montgomery Warren."

"How did you find all this out? I wasn't able to get any further than the birth and death dates," Marissa mused to herself. It had to be something like that, and now with the volume of poetry to confirm the existence of the person, a new writer and poet of worth would come forth from the United States. This was potentially a bombshell, which would reverberate through the literary world. No wonder the person who had Jeff kidnapped wanted the books. They were, indeed, worth millions.

"There were some other documents in the family of the estate you went to and when we started digging, we were able to uncover where other family members had researched the story. No real proof, just hearsay from the lawyer's family in England and then things that others surmised also," Stephen replied.

"Riinnnggg." They all jumped in their seats. "Rinnggg." Marissa reached for the receiver.

"Hello," she said.

"Marissa," Jeff's voice came through the phone, "I love you."

Marissa almost fainted again, so relieved was she to hear his voice. "Jeff, oh sweetheart, are you all right? Has he been treating you okay?"

"Honey, don't cry, I'm okay, my eyes are blindfolded, so I don't know where I am, but I am okay. Did you find the books?"

"Jeff, I just told him that so he would let me talk to you. Your message on the tape ran out before I could find out where you put them. Are they here in the house still?"

"Yes, on the shelves where I would have put them but in different jackets. I wanted to surprise you. I love you, Marissa, I can't talk any longer, he is pulling me away," Jeff finished.

"Marissa, I want those books delivered to me tomorrow at closing time at the city library. I want them put on the shelf in the poetry section and I will leave instructions in their place when I pick them up where you can find your husband. Is that clear? No tricks now or you will never see him again," the man growled.

"I understand, tomorrow, at the city library, at closing time." She hung up the phone and turned to look at Stephen and Elaine.

"I don't have much time to find those books."

Stephen, Elaine, and Marissa began again to look for the books.

"Jeff says he switched the jackets and the books are here somewhere in the house in different jackets," Marissa said.

The library shelves were filled to the overflowing with books in jackets. Some of the older volumes had no jackets at all. They could ignore them. So book by book, each one of them removing the covers and looking at the title on the front and author's name on the side, they began the search. This was going to take too long and they were going to have to have more help. Marissa decided that she was going to have to call her daughters and tell them what had happened. They were going to have to come and help them search for the books.

An hour or so after talking with them, her two girls arrived. They rolled up their sleeves and each took a section of the library and searched. A publisher has thousands of books of different titles and subjects, and they looked and looked and still no sign of the hidden books.

"Riinngg." The phone startled them into statues. "Riinngg." Marissa rushed to the table and answered. "Hello."

On the other end of the line, Donna answered, "The books you asked for are on the way, you owe us big time, but we love you and you tell us when you can."

"Oh, Donna, thank you, thank you so much." This would solve the problem of what to do tomorrow when she had to go to the pickup location, but they still needed to find the original books.

The night drew on and they worked without rest knowing that tomorrow would dawn with the decision of what to do. Marissa sat down for a few minutes to rest when the doorbell buzzed. What was it about her getting some rest that made the doorbell buzz? There on the porch stood the messenger from the publishing company. She reached for the package and closed the door.

Inside the box were the two volumes of poetry looking exactly like the missing books. You wouldn't be able to tell unless someone knew the poetry inside was different. But they both looked brand new and she knew her volume that had come from the auction was worn so she had to make one look older than the other did. She began to rub and rub at the front cover to take off some of the gold leaf of the title and putting lotion on her hands, she kneaded and held the volume over and over until the discoloration of age began to appear on the book.

Finally, she took the book and banged it on the edge of the table to rough the leather at the corners of the book.

"What do you guys think, does it look older than the other one?"

"It sure does, Mom," exclaimed her oldest daughter.

"Just one more finishing touch and I'm through," Marissa instructed.

"What is that?" Stephen asked.

"I need some dirt!"

"Dirt!"

"Yes, could someone go outside and get me some dirt?" Marisa asked as she walked to the kitchen to turn on the oven. "It hasn't quite got the patina that the other book had, it has to be dirtier."

She took the bowl full of dirt that Stephen had gotten from the back yard and crumbled it on a cookie sheet, and then she placed the dirt on the oven shelf and set the timer for 10 minutes. This has got to work, it just had to. She had to get Jeff back.

"Please don't stop what you are doing, keep looking for the books," she cried, "I can do this."

The timer went off and she turned off the oven. With a potholder, she carefully pulled the hot cookie sheet out and set it on the counter to cool.

Picking up the damaged book, she began again to rub the covers with her hand warming up the oils in the leather. Dipping her fingers into the dry dusty dirt, she rubbed the surfaces until they became greasy and crusted with grime, as they would have become over long years of use. Finally, when she was satisfied that the book looked as much like the original as she could get it, she set it aside to dry.

She went back into the library to help.

"Marissa, I think you should get some sleep," Elaine said, "you look worn down."

"Elaine is right, Mom, you go to bed, we will keep working all night if need be," Willow said.

"No, I want to help, I need to be doing something," she answered.

"I think that you all should get some rest," Stephen countered. "Why don't you all go home and come back tomorrow and we'll start again. Marissa, you get some rest, you will need it tomorrow, and you don't want Jeff to see you worn down, do you?"

"You're right, we all need rest," she said. "You girls go on home and come back tomorrow, we have until the public library closes, we'll finish this then. Just put a piece of paper where you stopped so we'll know where to start again."

One by one they hugged her and left until only she and Stephen were left standing in the hall.

"Marissa, I don't want you to worry anymore, everything will be all right. Tomorrow you will have Jeff back and everything will be as it was before, except..."

"What do you mean by, except?" Marissa asked.

"Except now you know you will also have me! I know you love Jeff and I am satisfied that you are happy but I want you to also know that I have never forgotten you and what you meant to me. I am always here for you, if you ever need me! There, I have said what needed to be said," and he gathered her into his arms and held her tightly for a few minutes before he turned and went through the door quietly closing it behind him.

What is happening to me, she wondered, what had she done to make Stephen think that there was still a chance for him? I love Jeff with all my heart, and yet I feel a kinship with Stephen still. How is it possible that he still cares for me? Why does he tell me this now? It is too much to think about, what can I tell him?

She slowly made her way to the bedroom and drew the curtains, throwing herself across the bed.

"Oh, Stephen, why must you tell me this now!"

She drifted into a troubled sleep, with images whirling in her head, first Jeff, and then Stephen's face, standing side by side.

CHAPTER FOURTEEN

November 1, 1847

Catherine had prevailed on Daniel to return Caroline to her home and they were preparing to leave Seacliff when she carried a parcel to give to Caroline. The month had flown by and they two women had grown ever closer. They had talked of baby names and nurses and nannies and good schools for later in their children's lives. It was as if they knew that decisions and desires needed to be stated now while they were both together.

"Caroline, will you do me this last favor when you arrive home? I do not have the address for Fredrika Bremer at home and I wish to send this parcel to her. Can you contact some of her friends or the rental agent who supplied her home and find out how to get in touch with her? I would be grateful. I would do it myself but obviously now I can not show myself in public. Please be a dear and do this for me."

"Of course, I will, I will see it gets in tomorrow's post. Now, young lady, you take good care of yourself and as soon as I can go about again, I will come to see you and then the children will be playing together while we watch. Oh the happy days ahead for you!" Caroline exclaimed.

But she was not so sure, there was something in the way Catherine carried the child that portended difficulties. She would speak to Daniel on the way home to warn him. They hugged again and then she and Daniel boarded the coach to the ferry jetty.

On the trip across the sound, Caroline confided to Daniel, "I fear for her, Daniel, keep a close eye and at the first sign of trouble send for the physicians. She is too isolated here at Seacliff. Would that I could get her to come to town and have help close at hand."

"I am sure you are mistaken, she seems in the best of health," he said, "but never fear I will not leave her side, of that you may be sure."

"Daniel, you are the one she should be betrothed to in truth. I tell you now that her husband will not come, in fact does not even know that there is a child being born." Caroline told all, so desperate was she for Catherine's happiness. "You must never let her know that I have told you this. It must come from her."

"I promise not to breathe a word of this to her, but I guessed as much. Catherine is a strong woman and I would expect nothing less than this. She would not give her heart lightly, but once given it would be forever given thus. We will have to see what the birth changes."

"Ha, she said as much herself. Well, I trust you to care for her and I will let you know the outcome of my travail. I am much recovered after my visit with you both and I feel that this month will go swiftly and surely. I long for the child I carry."

"Then worry no more and content yourself that all is well with Catherine too, I shall see it so." He took his leave of her as by this time they had arrived at the door of her home.

On his arrival back at Seacliff, he found Catherine again writing at her desk. When she had finished she turned and crossed the room to him. In her hand was a small volume, which she extended to him. "I wanted to give you something no one else could give you, a piece of myself. This book is the sum of my life to this time and represents all that is the best of my mind and heart. I hope you remember me with fondness when you read it."

He took the book and opened the fly page. There, in her hand, was a message intended just for him. As he read the words, he felt the mist gathering in his own eyes. The words leapt from the page and lingered in his heart. He touched her chin with his fingers and lifted her lips to his own. How could he give her up? She smiled at him while the misting in her eyes matched his.

"Now I have one final favor to ask of you," she said. "I have another volume that I need delivered, but I wish to wait until my child is come to send it. Will you take it for me then? I am sure that you may leave after the child is come and it will take some time to deliver."

"Of course, just tell me to whom and where it goes and I will see that it is done," he said.

"No, no, you must take it yourself, I would trust no one else," she said.

"Then, it will be done as you say, I will go myself. Now get your rest, you look a little tired this evening and we have talked a lot. We'll talk of this more at length when the time is nearer."

"Thank you, Daniel, I don't know what I would do without you, you are so kind." Catherine sighed and let herself be guided to the stairs and to her room.

November 13, 2001

The ringing phone next to Marissa's bed snapped her awake. She grabbed at the phone as she looked at the clock on the nightstand. 8:00 a.m. Can that be right, how could she have slept so long? She placed the receiver to her ear and heard, "Marissa, this is Stephen, I'm on the way over with breakfast. I will be there in 30 minutes unless traffic ties me up. Get yourself ready to eat something."

"I'm not hungry, I don't think I can eat anything."

"I know you are running on nervous energy, but that will run out soon and you need to eat. Now get dressed and I'll see you soon," he said as he severed the connection.

Why is he in such a hurry to get over here? I don't know what to say to him. Jumping in the shower, she hurried through her bath splashing water everywhere. After a thorough scrubbing, she climbed out and threw on some comfortable jeans and an old sweatshirt. She would not be accused of trying to dress up for him. Stepping off the bottom step, she heard the knock at the door. What is the matter with the doorbell? Then she remembered the alarm and ran to disable it. Peering through the window, she saw him holding bags and drink cups along with the morning paper.

"Where is your briefcase this morning?" she inquired. "Aren't we afraid that the kidnapper will wonder who you are coming here all the time?"

"Nope, we have the neighborhood staked out and any suspicious cars are being checked through license registration files back at the office. Are you hungry yet?"

"I could use a cup of that coffee you are holding and maybe if there is an egg sandwich in there I might be able to eat that. I don't suppose there is half a grapefruit, too."

Stephen laughed. "Nope, you just have to settle for coffee and donuts this time." Marissa wondered how he could be so sure of himself all the time. She almost never was, though she could put on a good show. Perhaps it was the badge, but then she remembered back in high school, when he was also so confident and she had felt safe with him.

"Are you ready to go back to work on the bookshelves? We still have a lot of books to go through and Jeff says there is a letter for me also written to my old married name. I don't know what it is all about but I am sure it can't be very important because Jeff and I have been married a long time now and everyone we know knows my married name and where we live. But keep an eye out for a letter addressed to Marissa Feinstein."

"Marissa, when we find the books, or if we have to use the dummy books you have made up, I want you to let me have a policewoman deliver them to the library. I think you should stay here with the girls. Just in case this character has something more sinister than just getting a hold of the books in mind."

"But he will know it's not me, I am sure he has seen me before, now that I think of it. In fact, I would be willing to bet that he is the same man who bid on the box of books against me at the action and also the same man who followed me when I left the restaurant the day I went to the library for research. So you see, it has to be me delivering the books, or he will know the police are in on it, and then, who knows what he might do to Jeff."

Stephen looked long and hard at Marissa. He couldn't argue with what she had said, but the feeling in the pit of his stomach told him he wouldn't survive it if something happened to this woman.

"All right, Marissa, but we will have the library filled with undercover cops inside and out. And don't argue with me on this, it isn't any use."

"Whatever you say, Stephen, you are the law and you guys know best how to handle this."

"Now back to work with us. The girls and Elaine will be here soon, I am sure, to help."

It wasn't long after that that Elaine and the girls did show up and the search began again in earnest. But even after checking every volume in the library, the book's hiding place remained a mystery.

Finally, the time arrived to take the dummy books to the location. Marissa put her jacket on and gathered up her car keys. Stephen turned and left the house through the living room door headed for his car.

"Mom, don't you want one of us to go with you?" Sandy argued.

"Honey, yes, I would like all of you to go with me, but, if I don't go alone something awful may happen to Daddy and we just can't let that happen. You stay here and I will be back as soon as I can."

Looking back one more time at them gathered in her library, she let herself out the kitchen door and opened the car door. Seated in the dark garage, she indeed wondered if she would be able to carry this off. She opened the overhead door and backed the car out.

The streets were dark with only the headlights reflecting off the windows to give light as she backed out of the driveway and headed down Tamerlane toward the city and the library. It was only a few miles, a drive that she had made many times in the past when she was doing research or just picking up items for the girls' school projects or for her book club. But the stillness of the night and the absence of other cars in the road and on the streets of the city made it feel sinister in some way. Where had her confidence in her surroundings gone? Why did just driving to the library make her uneasy? Jeff was her whole world, now she understood what it would be like to be truly alone without him in it. This just had to work. There wasn't anything else to try. She wondered who was behind all this, surely not the man whom she had seen at the auction. If it was him, why hadn't he just outbid her for the book? Unless, he had been told not to draw too much attention to it there. And who was the woman who had called Jeff the night of the accident? Perhaps she was the one who had hired the kidnapper or at least was in on the conspiracy. They must be getting paid a lot to stick their necks out like this. Kidnapping is a capital crime; if caught they would spend most of their lives in jail. The thought made her even more uneasy. Someone facing that kind of punishment would not hesitate to get rid of any witnesses and Jeff might be able to help the police catch them. Oh, dear Lord, don't let anything happen to Jeff.

There, ahead was the library, and the parking lot was almost empty. It was usually filled with cars, but it was close to closing time. She would get this done and get back to her girls. She hoped the police were ready for this fellow. They would only have one chance to nab him. She hoped she didn't screw it up somehow.

Hurrying up the steps, she pulled the large ornate door of the library open and walked inside. She remembered now, he had said upstairs on the second floor, in the second to last aisle on the right, the poetry section, to put them on the third shelf down from the top. Yes, there's the stairs to the second floor. She looked around to see if she could spot him. She saw several people at tables and in chairs, looking through books, but no sign of the kidnapper. When she reached the second floor, she began searching for the correct location. There it was now, the third shelf down from the top, and there were the works of Browning and Poe right here on this shelf! Yes, her volumes would be very comfortable resting here with these literary giants. She placed the books on the shelf and turned to retrace her steps to the first floor. There had been no note but she guessed he meant it about not giving information until he had the books. The police would just have to do their thing now; she had done all she could.

Marissa returned to her car and pulled out of the parking lot. The drive home wasn't much easier for her, she had always liked to be in control of every situation and now she had given up all control and handed it over to Stephen and the police force. It was hard for her to wait. The girls were waiting in the hallway when she let herself back in the house; she looked to see if Stephen was still there. No, he had gone to take up the watch with the others at the library. She hadn't seen him leave before she did. She sat down on the couch and began to pray, gathering all the girls and Elaine to her while she silently sent her thoughts to God to help her.

The librarian was turning out the lights, meanwhile, back at the library. She was preparing to leave for the evening. She snapped the last light out and pulled open the heavy self-locking door to leave the building. Stepping out on to the stairs, she heard the door close with a click behind her. Now the library was thrown into darkness with the only light that of the emergency exit light still burning over the exit doors. Quiet settled over the building. Nothing was moving, except the soft hum of the fans from the heating plant. Suddenly, a flashlight began to play across the floor leading to the stairs. The noiseless footsteps of the intruder climbed stealthily to the second floor, playing the light back and forth across the aisles of books until he came to the correct one. Yes, there they were, the volumes she had brought. Now to place the note and get out of here. He shoved a piece of paper in their place and slipped the books of poetry into the inside pocket of his coat. Then he snapped off the flashlight and retreated the way he came, quietly and quickly. As he reached the first floor and was almost to the door, all the lights were switched back on and a voice yelled from the shadows, "Stop, don't move."

He tried to make it to the door but was tackled from behind and wrestled to the ground. With his hands jerked behind his back, he felt the handcuffs on his wrists. Then he was turned over and lifted to his feet. There he stood facing his attacker.

"You have the right to remain silent. You have the right to an attorney. If you can't afford an attorney, the court will appoint one for you. If you waive that right, anything you say or do can be used in court of law. Now where is Jeffery Delclare? And you better not lie; you are in enough trouble already. If anything happens to Delclare, you will go up for murder." Stephen was panting from the exertion as he questioned the offender.

"He is okay, just tied and blindfolded, maybe a little weak, but I haven't hurt him. I told his wife, I would turn him over after I got the books and I have."

"There are directions here, Detective McGuire, we found them on the shelf," said the another officer who had searched the shelves.

"Okay, some of you others take this guy back to the office and book him, I am going with you to get Delclare," Stephen replied. "Let's go, and don't spare the sirens, I want Delclare in the hospital as soon as yesterday."

October 20, 1847

Catherine rose early and began to write. The mornings were always the best time for her writing and she began to feel the verse flow, this time almost like a lullaby to her unborn child. They were already so close; she would have long talks with her child every day and sometimes when the discussion was about something especially nice, she would feel a gentle kick in the side as if her child was answering her. She knew that this child would be a companion and helpmate to her in the future years and she hoped that he or she would know its father as she had never known hers.

It was nearing the end of November and she was sure that she should hear soon of Caroline. Surely there was nothing amiss. If she didn't hear soon, she would insist that Daniel go and inquire. These days childbirth could often carry complications.

She rang for the maid and had her build up the fire in the fireplace. The chill was in the air and she didn't seem to be able to keep warm any more. That was unusual for her, as she had always been robust. But there, the warmth was spreading through her now. Ah, that was better. As the maid turned to go, Catherine called to her, "Inquire if Mr. Graves has had his breakfast yet. If not, lay a place for me today, I feel much better and would take mine with him if it is not too early for him." The last few days she had not felt like coming down to breakfast and had had a tray sent up. She didn't want to worry Daniel unduly, so it would be better to go down if she felt like it at all.

Shortly she dressed and made her way downstairs to the conservatory. She liked to have her meals there when the weather wasn't too inclement and today promised to be fair. It had been nasty up to now with storms blowing and roaring surfs, but today the clouds were puffy and the sea calmer. The winds had abated and the warmth from the dining room fireplace flowed into the room and filled the spaces with heat. She sat down at the table and waited for Daniel to appear. Why was she so tired? Of course, she was pregnant but were pregnant women always so tired in the seventh month? She knew that Caroline had been unwell, but she put that down to her age at carrying a first child. Now she could hardly hold a pen and the effort to trot around the gardens was almost more than she could handle.

"Good morning, Cathy," Daniel said, as he entered the room. "I am glad you are feeling better today. I have missed your smiling face at breakfast these last few days. I hope you are not truly sick. Perhaps I should fetch the physician to examine you."

"Don't be silly, I am indulging myself, that is all. Making everyone wait on me and treat me tenderly. It's all a ruse. Don't you know I am a consummate actress?" She laughed.

But he looked closely at her and saw the beginnings of the shadows under her eyes and wondered. Should he get the physician? Would she be upset if he did it without her permission? Better not to rock the boat. Perhaps if she were given a few more days, she would bounce back to her old self. If she weren't better soon, though he would surely insist. He had seen pregnant women before in his tenants and most of them stayed in fine health all the way through their time. Some women had a harder time and perhaps this was Cathy's fate. He prayed it wouldn't be so.

She saw him watching her and needed to get his mind off of her so she quickly changed the subject.

"Daniel, I am wondering why we have not heard of Caroline's condition. Do you think anything is wrong? If we do not hear by the first week of November, you must go and inquire of her for me. Captain Smith's ship will be back in port by now and he will surely have word for you of her. I am so anxious to learn what she had, boy or girl. Would you go for me next week?"

"If you will be all right here while I am gone, I will, but if you seem sicker than you are, then you must accompany me to the doctor's. Then we will go round to see her together. You will still be able to travel then," Daniel insisted.

"Oh, I can't leave Seacliff before the baby is born. I have not been to the city since I found out I was pregnant."

"And why not? Plenty of pregnant woman go abroad these days, didn't Caroline come here and she was 7 months at the time?"

"Not for me, it is different. I can't explain, but it is."

"All right, but mark my words, if you are sicker, you will go, if I have to carry you myself!"

"I will be fine, you are not to worry. I am going to be just fine."

CHAPTER FIFTEEN

November 13, 2001, 9:15 p.m.

The sirens' wailing could be heard cutting through the night as Stephen and the other officers roared across the city until they reached the outskirts on the opposite side of town from where Marissa waited with her daughters and Elaine. Reaching the city limits, they kept going into the countryside. The directions were scribbled in horrible writing but it looked as though the trail was leading into the next county.

Calling the county sheriff of that county on the radio, Stephen requested backup and a clearer instruction on how to reach the place the paper had described. The man had indicated a County Road J, and then go six miles until you came to the second dirt lane on the left side of the highway. Go down that 1/2 mile and you would see an old farmhouse surrounded by grazing cows. The sheriff of Omaise County thought a second. That sounded like the old Sheppard place that was used for grain storage and cattle grazing. Nobody lived there now; there weren't even any neighbors for a couple of miles in either direction. He agreed to get out there and wait for Stephen before he did anything and he would keep a look out for any vehicles parked around just in case this fellow had had an accomplice. They still had about a thirty-minute drive. Best to shut down the sirens and make a quiet approach.

There was County Road J, now a left and six miles, there, there is a dirt lane on the left, now the next dirt lane should be it. Stephen mentally kept tabs on the directions while his driver turned the corner and slowed to a crawl down the dirt road. Too fast and the dirt would fly and perhaps be seen, the moon had come up now and there was more light to discern things by. There ahead, he could see it, a farmhouse with farm fences around it and cattle lying around on the ground or up chewing their cud. Over there to the right was another squad car with the Omaise County Sheriff insignia on it. He walked to the car to speak to the sheriff.

"Anything moving around here, sheriff?" He got out his badge to identify himself. "Detective Stephen McGuire."

"Nope, we been here about fifteen minutes and it's as quiet as a churchyard, if you know what I mean."

"I know what you mean and I don't like the sound of it. Let's go in and see what we have here."

They slowly approached the house, people at the back and front watching for signs of life. Stephen pulled out his flashlight and bullhorn.

"If there is anyone in that house, you had better come out now with your hands up before we come in after you." There was no response. Stephen stepped up on the rotten porch with the boards creaking under his feet and slowly pushed open the door. He showed his flashlight over the inside of the house. In the kitchen were the remains of some kind of fast food that had been eaten and then left to draw insects. He walked into the other room and finding nothing continued to search until he came to the bathroom. The door was closed, he nudged it open with his foot, and there, sitting in the bathtub, blindfolded, with his hands and feet tied, and duck tape across his mouth, was Jeffery Delclare.

Stephen crossed the room to him and leaned down to take the blindfold off and the tape off his mouth.

"Thank God, I thought I was going to be left here to die. I have never been so glad to see anyone in my life."

"Take it easy, Mr. Delclare, let me get these things off your hands and feet."

He leaned down with his pocketknife and began cutting the plastic ties that had bound Jeff and were cutting into the flesh of his wrists and ankles. Stephen turned his head and shouted for someone to come and help him lift Delclare out of the tub and carry him to the squad car. They got him settled in the back seat and motioned the neighboring county sheriff over.

"I am going to get him back to our hospital as fast as I can. Thanks for all your help, Sheriff."

"No problem, glad we could be of help. Oh, by the way, one of my men found this laying on the floor of the kitchen," he replied. "Thought you might need it for fingerprints or something." Stephen took the piece of paper and carefully placed it in a plastic bag and put it into his pocket. Then he gestured to the driver to take off.

Stephen looked in the back seat; Jeffery Delclare had slumped down on the seat only his head showing from under the blankets Stephen had covered him with. He looked exhausted; he needed sleep and heat. They turned on the sirens and turned up the heater and headed for the hospital as fast as they could. It was faster than waiting for an ambulance to get there and there was nothing to do for him but to get him to help as fast as possible.

He hoped there was nothing more than exhaustion wrong with him for Marissa's sake.

November 1847

The drive along the coast to the ferry jetty was cold and windy with a hint of the winter that would be descending soon. Already New York City had had some snow, though the afternoon warmth and the paving stones of the cities had melted it before it had much of a chance to pile up. Daniel pulled his coat closer around his neck and nestled back against the back of the coach. It would be a cold ferry ride, too. He hoped this wasn't a fool's errand and that there was good news for Cathy when he returned. She had looked no worse when he left and so decided he could safely leave her while he inquired for her friend Caroline. But he would be glad to finish it and return to her side as quickly as he could.

He boarded the ferry and sought someplace out of the wind to make the crossing; it would not be very much longer before the ferry would stop running for the winter. He hoped that Catherine had had the baby before it did. He had no experience in delivering a child and the doctor would have to be on hand for this delivery. He did not understand why she would not leave Seacliff. She could easily afford to move into the city to have the baby and then return when the weather had moderated and the ferry resumed its regular schedule. But no, she would not leave Seacliff. She was waiting until after the birth. Why the stubbornness to wait there? Couldn't the waiting be done anywhere? Women, when did men ever understand the workings of their hearts or minds? Certainly, he did not.

He spent his time on the ferry trip mulling over these things in his mind. Soon enough, the other side was reached, and he found a cab to deliver him to the Smiths' home. He climbed the steps with instructions to the cabby to wait until he made sure his welcome. *Knock, Knock.* He waited at the door. Abruptly, the door was flung open and a wild-eyed man grabbed him by the collar and pulled him inside.

"My God man, what has kept you so long? We sent for you this morning for my wife, are you daft that you waited this long? Now get upstairs and help her, you incompetent fool!" the man shouted.

"I am sorry, sir, but you mistake me for someone else. We have never met, let me introduce myself. I am Daniel Graves and I'm come at Catherine Barrett's insistence to inquire for Mrs. Caroline Smith's health. My word, sir, get hold of yourself."

"You mean, you are not the doctor?"

"No, to be sure, I am not, are you expecting a doctor? Surely Mrs. Caroline is not ill."

"No, she's not ill, she is delivering at this moment and the doctor has not come, do you know anything about it, sir?" Captain wailed.

Just then the rap came again at the door, and without waiting for Daniel to answer, he flung wide the door and pulled the man standing there into the room.

"Dr. Brent, I hope."

"Yes, I am Dr. Brent, and I believe someone called for me. What is wrong?"

"My wife, my wife needs you. She is in labor and is having a most difficult time, please let me take you to her at once." Captain Smith rushed off with the doctor in tow and left Daniel standing in the hall aghast at it all. So this was how the doctors behaved in this country. He would have to have a word with this doctor before he left this place and see if there was anything that he himself could do while waiting for the doctor to arrive when Catherine went into labor. Yes, he wouldn't leave here without talking with the doctor for sure.

Shortly, Captain Smith returned to take Daniel's coat and take him to the parlor. He apologized profusely and of course Daniel told him to give it no thought, it was a reasonable mistake, he had been expecting a doctor and not expecting anyone else. Daniel must have appeared just at the very worst time. But now they would have news for Catherine on Daniel's return and he hoped that the news if it could be good would cheer her and set her mind at rest.

And, indeed, good news it was, when several hours later the doctor came to tell Captain Smith that he had a healthy, beautiful baby daughter. The captain was overjoyed that his wife had survived the ordeal and that now there were two women to baby him in his old age. They toasted the child and Daniel took a peek at Caroline to satisfy his curiosity that she was, without doubt, all right. She reclined on pillows and was wearily smoothing her daughter's blond hair back away from her face while the child suckled at her breast. The picture tore at Daniel's heart. Someday he would like to see a child of his suckle at Catherine's breast. Would that ever happen for him?

The doctor came to get his fee and Daniel stopped him in the hall.

"Doctor, I am presently staying out at Seacliff and I believe my hostess is a patient of yours who is expecting?"

"Yes, and what is your hostess' name?"

"Catherine Barrett-Poe."

"Oh yes, a late December date as I remember. And how is she faring? I expected to see her before the delivery date. I am surprised she has not kept the appointments."

"I cannot convince her to leave Seacliff. Doctor, when we need you I will send a coachman for you with instructions for you to be brought to Seacliff, but if something happens that you can not get there, what can I do, if anything, to help my friend?"

"Man, I don't think there is anything that you could do, but ask the house servants if there is a midwife in the neighborhood or among the household servants and rely on them to do the helping until I come."

"All right. I will do my best to stay out of the way or help in anyway I can."

"Don't worry, man, babies have been getting themselves born since the world began and they will continue to do so."

The doctor took his payment and left the house. Shortly afterwards, Daniel took his leave from Captain Smith and started on his return to Seacliff.

November 13, 2001
Waiting for Word that Night

Back in the house on Tamerlane Drive, Marissa sat at her desk in the library with a pad and pen to try to explain to Stephen how much she valued his friendship and his help. How grateful she would always be for all the support and love that he continued to show her. How could she make him understand now that Jeff would shortly be returned to her, that Jeff and Jeff alone had her love and devotion? She would put Stephen from her thoughts, assign him to the past where he belonged. As usual the words began to flow and fly onto the paper in verse form. At the end of the composition, she folded it and placed it in an envelope addressed to Stephen McGuire at the sheriff's office. She put a stamp on it and walked outside to put it in the mailbox.

When she returned to the kitchen, she called to the girls and Elaine, "You girls feel like a cup of coffee? I am going to make some, I need to stay focused and awake."

"Sure, Mom, if you are going to have some," Willow replied.

"Now where is that coffee can? Elaine, you put things away differently than I do." She began rummaging around in her cupboard, and noticed one of her cookbooks out of order. She didn't remember a cookbook with a dust jacket on it. What was that doing in here? She lifted the book down from the shelf and examined it. When she removed the dust cover, she couldn't believe her eyes. There inside the cookbook dust cover were the two books of poetry that they had been searching for.

There also was the letter that Jeff had mentioned. Yes, it was addressed to Marissa Feinstein. Who could it be from? She took her finger and lifted the flap on the envelope. What was this? A letter from Stephen, why hadn't he mentioned it? She sat down at the kitchen table and began to read.

> *My dear Marissa,*
>
> *I know you will be surprised to receive a letter from me after all these years, but I have wanted to get in touch with you for a long time. When I was back home last month, I asked my folks if they knew anything about your family. They told me about your brother. I am so sorry to hear about his passing, I know how much you must miss him.*
>
> *Perhaps you would like to have lunch sometime, just for old time's sake. Just give me a ring at the number on the enclosed card and we can set up a time.*
>
> *Affectionately,*
> *Steve*

Attached to the letter was a card with the number of the sheriff's office, which she had called the night Jeff disappeared.

"Riinngg." The phone broke the silence of the room. "Rinngg." In the living room, the girls waited to hear if their mother was picking up. No more rings, which meant she had picked up the receiver. Both girls gathered at the door of the living room waiting for their mother to come out of the kitchen.

When she came around the corner of the kitchen door, her eyes were shining and her smile threatened to outdo the sun.

"Your father is on his way to the hospital. He's okay, they think, just weak, tired, and cold and we are on our way, too. Get your things and cars and follow me or come with me," Marissa cried.

"Elaine, can you lock up for me? I know you must want to get home to your husband, too. I can't thank you enough for all you've done for me." Marissa ran to her friend and hugged her tight.

"Go on now and get going, I'll take care of everything here," Elaine said. Marissa raced to her car and jumped in. The garage door slammed up as she threw the car in reverse and squealed the tires out of the garage. Marissa was in a hurry to get to the hospital, in a hurry to end the nightmare of the last few days.

Elaine walked into the kitchen to turn off the coffeepot and tidy up. She looked down at the kitchen table where the envelope and letter from Stephen lay forgotten in the excitement of the phone call. She picked it up, read it, and then shaking her head slightly side to side, she folded it and placed it in her purse. No need for this to be here when Jeff came home. She set the alarm and closed the door behind her.

The emergency room was filled with people when Marissa arrived, there were police standing everywhere smiling at her. Sandy and Willow rushed up to the nurse at the desk and asked to see Mr. Jeffery Delclare. They were shown into the emergency room to a cubicle with the curtains drawn around it. Marissa was almost afraid to draw the curtains back, afraid of what she was going to see. As she reached out, pulling it back, she saw Stephen standing at the side of Jeff's bed asking him questions. Both men looked up at her as she pulled the curtains back.

"Honey, this is Detective Stephen McGuire and he has just saved my life. You will never know how grateful we both are, Detective McGuire!" Jeff exclaimed.

"Yes, we certainly are, Detective McGuire," Marissa seconded as she looked intently into his eyes. Stephen looked at Marissa and then at Jeff.

His face barely registered the pain that he felt inside. He knew this was the way it should be. He knew that he had missed his chance, though he would never understand why or how it had happened. It was time for him to go.

"It's what I get paid to do, sir. I am happy we had a successful conclusion in your case." He picked up his coat and walked toward the door.

"Marissa, I don't know how much I can protect you, but this time you did a great job of protecting me. Detective McGuire told me how you figured out a plan for fixing dummy books and had a poem all ready to read to him that you thought I had given you in a dream. You are amazing."

How had she known about the poem? Jeff wondered as he lay watching the emotions play on her face. There had always seemed to be an invisible thread that held the two of them together, something so intangible, so gossamer, yet so strong that it had weathered separations and near-death experiences to emerge stronger than before.

"No, we are amazing, honey. We are a team. We have always been on the same wavelength. That is why I get so uneasy when you are in danger, you are the other end of my safety line," she said. "Just don't ever scare me like this again."

"Believe me, I didn't have anything to do with it. But someday I will be gone, honey, you have to face it and go on. Now, at last, I think you will be able to. The things you have weathered in the last two days would have destroyed a lesser person."

"Perhaps, but I don't have to think about that now. And incidentally, why would you put a poetry book in a cookbook dust jacket of all things," she chided.

"Oh, then, you did find them." Jeff laughed.

"Yes, but why there? You know I rarely cook anymore."

"Maybe a subtle hint for a quiet candlelight dinner like the old days."

"Oh you! You are incorrigible, but I love you. When can you go home?"

"Right now," he said, "get the nurse to give me the necessary papers, I am signing myself out right now."

He signed the necessary papers with a promise to call his regular doctor on the next day and left with his wife and children gathered around him. At the curb each of the girls kissed and hugged their father and mother and left to return to their own families.

Jeff settled into the passenger seat of the car and turned his head to watch as Marissa slowly eased the car into reverse to leave the parking spot and move into the street on the way to Tamerlane Drive and home.

CHAPTER SIXTEEN

That Night

The house stood empty and quiet as they came up the long winding driveway toward it. So strange to know that even now there might still be someone out there who wanted them harmed. Surely Stephen would be able to get the information he needed from the kidnapper on who else would be involved. She knew that the police were somewhere here, the surveillance had not been lifted yet. She touched the garage door opener and pulled the car inside closing it behind her. They crossed to the kitchen door and let themselves in, disarming the alarm behind them. But Marissa reset it as soon as they had both gotten inside. She still felt the necessity of being careful. She needed a nightcap and a soak after the events of the past 24 hours. And she knew that Jeff needed food and rest, so she turned to him and asked, "What will it be, coffee, ham and eggs, or wine and cheese and crackers and bed?"

"The coffee menu sounds good, but I don't want you to cook now, I'll settle for wine, cheese and crackers followed by bed," he said.

"Go into the library and settle yourself and I'll bring it in on a tray." She busied herself in the kitchen and then with a laden tray and the two books of poetry beside, she followed Jeff into the library. He was seated on the loveseat and patted the place beside him. She grabbed a small table from beside another chair and put the tray atop it. Jeff poured two glasses of red wine and took a slice of cheese on top a cracker. Marissa picked up the two poetry books that she had found right before the news came that Jeff had been found. She looked again at the one which she bought at auction and then at the one Jeff had had sent from the office. They were the same books, almost. She looked closely at each page, one after another to see if she could find the difference. They looked alike, but wait a minute, there was something different about the cover.

On the back cover of the older dirtier book there looked like a bulge between the pasted-on page of the leather wrapper. She showed it to Jeff.

"Is there something inside here, something hidden under this paper that is glued down?" she asked.

"Let's see," he said, and took a letter opener from the desk drawer and carefully slit the paper at the top of the book. "I think there is something in here." He pushed against the bulge from the bottom and it started to slip toward the slit in the top. Slowly another piece of folded paper emerged, and after carefully unfolding the document, it appeared to be a birth certificate parchment and a short letter. On the parchment appeared the name: "Jonathan Lee Poe born December 30, 1847, to Catherine Aurora Barret and Edgar Allan Poe."

Marissa picked up the letter and began to read,

> *"Dear Edgar,*
>
> *I know you are unaware of your son and so I enclose the birth certificate that the doctor has filled out for me, which I know you will safeguard. Please do not be angry with me for taking your name. I knew we would be married if you had known of the existence of Jonathan. I wanted you to come to me of your own accord and not because you felt a fatherly duty to your son and me. And so I did not write before now. Please care for him if anything should happen to me. Remember my love for you is 'timeless.' Yours forever, Cathy"*

"Oh, Jeff, how awful, she never delivered the book to him or he never found the letter!" Marissa cried.

"Yes, what a sad ending to a sad life. It might have made all the difference in Edgar," Jeff replied.

"Jeff, I hope I never forget to tell you every day how much I love you." Marissa sighed.

"Nor I you, sweetheart, now let's go upstairs and seal that with a kiss."

"Yes, my love."

November 30, 1847

Catherine had been expecting Daniel's return for hours and was beginning to think that the weather might have turned and he wouldn't make it back tonight, when the coach pulled up to the door and Daniel ran to the front door to be admitted. The weather had indeed turned bitter with chilling winds and biting bits of sleet being driven before them. It had been too much to hope that the good weather would last until the New Year. There was no help for it; they would just have to wait it out here at Seacliff.

Daniel came stamping the ice from his feet as he crossed the hall, scattering droplets on the carpets and slate entryway as he came. "Burr, it is getting wicked out there, my dear. We must be grateful we have a warm fire to sit before. I pity the poor people on the seas tonight." He lifted her chin to look in her eyes. She still looked a little pale but her eyes were sparkling and bright in the firelight. He kissed her on the cheek and she waited for his report on Caroline.

"I am sorry to send you in such weather, I had no idea it would turn so abruptly. Last year, the weather stayed fine all the way to Christmas. I felt the same would be true this year. I guess one can never depend on the weather. Like many people, it can be changeable."

"You can depend on me, I will never change the way I feel about you, Cathy," Daniel insisted.

"I am depending on you, in case you hadn't noticed, but I feel it is unfair to you and I impose unduly on you. You should be seeing the country and here you are constant companion to one who cannot even entertain you with other faces."

"I don't need another face but yours," he said.

She looked at the floor for a moment and then said, "What news of the city have you brought me? I am sitting on pins and needles to hear. What of Caroline?"

"Well," he laughed, "I was mistaken for the doctor when I arrived as Caroline had already been in labor twelve hours when I got there, and Captain Smith was distraught beyond repair. I thought I was going to be pressed into service to deliver, but no sooner had I been dragged into the house, the knock came and the door opened to the true doctor. Well, I was relieved, I can tell you, because I know not the first thing about babies or how they're born or anything."

"Oh my, what a surprise for you and them, and Caroline, is she delivered then?"

"Yes, of course, and they have a beautiful baby daughter. I did not stay to learn the name but you will doubtless have a visit when you are finished with your lying in."

"A baby girl, how wonderful. And what does she look like?" she asked.

"Tons of blonde hair and the bluest eyes I have ever seen, otherwise like any other baby I expect," he said.

"Oh, you men, you never notice anything except what you can see right out!" Catherine exclaimed.

"I expect that is so. I have often been told I was not very observant."

Catherine sat staring at the fire. A baby girl, how wonderful for Caroline, and she was sure that the captain would be pleased. A baby girl, someone for her daughter or son to play with and grow up with. How she would enjoy buying sweet things for Caroline's daughter. And as she sat musing on these things, Daniel watched the expressions play across her face. She was half smiling and he knew that she was thinking of the child of her friend. It had been worth the trip to see the happy relaxed look on her face. As if some of the worry about Caroline had taken away the worry about herself, as if she thought, if Caroline can do it at her age, I can surely do it too.

And, true enough, through the next weeks she rallied and became the old Catherine with the energy that he had once witnessed in England. They again started walking along the cliff edge to watch the sea, and down the drive toward the jetty. The calendar was getting shorter and shorter as it drew near to Christmas and the servants brought in the greens to liven up the dreary winter look of the house and a small celebration was planned for them.

It was during one such planning session that Daniel took the maid aside and inquired if any of the staff had knowledge of midwifery. While one or two had had children of their own, they would not own to any ability in the delivery of one, though they did mention an older women in the village who had helped them. He extracted a promise that they would have her fetched when the time came for Catherine's delivery. Everyone knew that it was getting close. Catherine was carrying the child lower and lower, but she seemed to have endless energy these days and was writing cards to send to friends and making decorations for the enormous fir tree that they had erected in the center of the conservatory. It was covered with small candles that they would light on Christmas Eve and then again on New Year's Eve to bring in the new year.

172

Catherine was enjoying having someone here to enjoy the holidays with her. The last year had seen her just into the house and she had had no time to decorate or be festive. This was a grand holiday this year and she was getting the best Christmas present in the world. She would have a child.

Christmas Eve was a wonderful occasion with the servants gathered around the conservatory walls to receive their gifts with Daniel on a long ladder with a very long taper lighting all the candles on the tree. The tree glowed in the night sky outside the glass windows of the conservatory as though a lighthouse for the ships at sea. Catherine gave to each of the staff a sum of money as a Christmas bonus and some small poem. Finished, they bid the mistress Merry Christmas and took their leave to go home to their families.

Daniel and Cathy watched until they were forced to put out the candles to keep from burning down the lovely tree. And then Cathy handed Daniel a folded piece of paper. "It is not much," she said, "but it is truly felt and meant." And on the paper were these words:

And One of You Are There

What does the future hold for me?
I neither know nor care
As long as one of those whom
I have loved along life's way is there.

As long as one of you are there.

The days unfold and I am led
Down the path that I must go
With stumbling, faltering, trembling feet
Which have now begun to slow.

Still one of you is there.

But a lighter heart still lives
Within this crumbling shell
While listening to the music
Of a lovely lilting bell.

When one of you are there.

The music Memory plays
Is sweet honey to the ears
Full of youth and joy and tears
Replayed throughout the years.

While one of you are there.

So day by day I listen
While the sands of time run on.
Bringing back the love I've known
And once have smiled upon.

And one of you is there.

Daniel took her in his arms, with tears in his eyes, and held her against his chest. This woman had such passion in her writing, could reach into his very soul and play on it like a harp. He felt as though love for her would well into his throat and choke him, so real was his emotion.

"Merry Christmas, Daniel," she said.

"Merry Christmas, Cathy."

It had only been three days. Cathy couldn't believe that Christmas was already three days behind them and now she had to ready the house for New Year's. A small celebration, no servants, they would fix the wassail toast and have the feast spread early so the staff could be away for their own entertainment. She was musing on this, when the first pain hit her. It was only a tightening, only that, nothing to be alarmed about. And so she continued to issue instructions to first this maid and that cook, until again she felt the tightening and this time the old cramping discomfort she remembered from so long ago. Nine months can make one forget, almost, the unpleasant monthly business and so she had, almost. But there less than ten minutes more and now another one came rolling over her.

She summoned the maid to ask Mr. Daniel if he could join her in the conservatory. He was in the library, she thought. He had become a great reader during his months' stay with her and often she would see him with the volume she had given him, reading at the window's light.

He came at once, concerned, for he knew she liked her household business to be uninterrupted and so he always took his leave of her while she handled these things.

"Cathy, the maid said you wanted me. What can I do for you, my love?" he asked.

"Daniel, I fear the child will be here before the New Year, you best send for the doctor for me," she replied as her face drew up in pain once again. "And have my maid help me up to bed, please."

Daniel scooped her up as she stood and carried her upstairs to her bedroom on the second floor. The bedroom was turned down for the night and so he lay her there and went to fetch the maids.

"Your mistress is come to the labor point, send the coachman for the doctor in the city right away and have a coach waiting at this side of the ferry for their return. Also send someone to the village to fetch the midwife there. Hurry, hurry, I don't know how long this will take, but we don't want to take chances and wait." Then, he sent two of them to care for Catherine and he began his wait.

It was several hours gone by, coming on to nightfall and still the doctor had not come. The sounds reaching him from the floor above were not those he wanted to hear. As the crescendo of pain spiraled ever higher, Daniel began to pace the conservatory floor, and then crossed to the hallway to check the drive to the jetty, over and over again he made the trip. When would the doctor arrive, surely he was on his way by now? The darkness was stealing in from the east as the winter sun slowly set over New York City and he could see from the hallway windows that the lights were being lit in the gaslights of the city. Again, those ripping cries of pain from up above. How long could she endure this? The midwife came forth every once in a while and shouted commands to the maids to do this and ready that, but still no cry of babe could be heard.

He paced to the conservatory again and sat at Cathy's desk, putting his head in his hands. He felt so helpless. How did they do it, these women who bore immense families? Why was there ever more than one child born to a family? If he were a woman, he would surely not go through it more than once. And then only because he did not know what was coming. A loud "Knock, knock, knock," came at the front door and he rushed to open it. And just as the captain had done before, he grabbed the doctor standing there and pulled him into the room. "Come on, man, see to her, she is suffering so!" he shouted.

"Don't worry, she must endure as they all endure. But let me go and I will see to it, don't worry." He took the stairs two at a time and opened the door of the room. The midwife met him at the door with a worried look on her face.

"The child is breech, I am afraid for her," she said.

"Oh good heavens, well, let us see what can be done." He motioned for hot water and handed the maid an instrument with instructions to wash and boil it well, and to return it to him as soon as possible.

Meanwhile, downstairs, Daniel again began his pacing, up and down, up and down. It seemed an eternity until he heard a slap and then a weak cry. And then silence. It was sometime later that the doctor descended the staircase rolling down his bloody sleeves. The look on his face was unreadable and Daniel rushed to him to hear the news.

"She is all right now, isn't she?" he cried, "I heard the babe cry, it's all over, isn't it?"

"Yes, the babe is born, but there were complications. The boy was breech and I had to cut and open her to bring him forth. Even at that it was necessary to use the forceps. She has lost a lot of blood and is very weak. She will not be able to nurse the child and I have arranged with the maids to find a wet nurse for him. But that is the least of our problems. She must rest and recover and I have forbidden her to get out of bed."

"Can I see her?" he asked.

"Yes, but do not tire her unduly."

The doctor took some paper from his pocket and headed toward the desk. He sat filling the forms out as she had instructed him. When he was finished, he folded the paper and prepared to climb the stairs again.

When he opened the door to her room, all had been tidied and put in good order; the baby lay in a cradle near to Catherine's bed, as she couldn't bear to be separated too far from him. The doctor checked him another time to make sure that he was not in any distress, and then crossed to the bed where Catherine lay with Daniel holding her hands.

"Now, remember Mrs. Poe, not one foot out of that bed until I have been back to see you, and that will be a week from today. Remember what I said, seven days in that bed, or I can't say how your recovery will go. See that she behaves. The wet nurse will be here shortly, and I have given instructions that she is to make her bed in the next room to hear the child if he should cry, so you are not get up even then."

He handed the paper to Catherine and she smiled weakly at him.

"I understand, doctor, and I will be good, really I will. Can I hold my baby, though, if I stay here in bed?"

"Well, of course, you can and should. And if your milk flows do not worry or try and nurse him. I want you to save all the strength you have for yourself. I will give you this powder which should help to dry you up. Take it before sleep tonight," he said.

"Yes, doctor, I will. And thank you so much," Catherine answered.

"You're welcome." He and Daniel left her to rest and went toward the front hall.

"Doctor, won't you stay and rest the night with us and leave again in the morning?"

"It is morning, man, and I have just time to make the first ferry of the day. I have other patients I must see to today," he said. "See that she eats something at daylight but small amounts and often during the day today. We will just have to see how each day goes. I will see you in a week. Good luck, young man."

With that he shrugged into his coat and went to the coach. With a wave of his hand, they pulled away toward the jetty.

Daniel gave instructions to the servant that Catherine was to have warm broth at daylight in small amounts and to continue that regiment every hour during the next day. And they were to wake him if she seemed worse. He then went to this room and collapsed across the bed.

It was noon before Daniel awoke with sunlight streaming in his windows and onto his face. He started at the brightness and groaned as every muscle screamed in protest. He had lain where he had fallen fully dressed and not moved an inch.

His stomach rumbled unmercifully and he knew that he would have to eat himself or he would be down in bed as well as she.

There by the fireplace was the morning meal, which had grown cold from waiting, and he crossed to it. But that didn't look very appetizing now and he crossed to the door and motioned to the maid passing by to take it away and he would come down to the dining room for something hot. "How is your mistress this morning?" he inquired.

"Oh, she slept the sleep of the dead until just an hour ago and then we started on the meals that you had ordered. She bade me keep watch until you woke and asked after you had eaten, you must come and visit her now that she was an invalid and could not leave her room."

"Tell her that just as soon as I have taken nourishment, I will come to her," he said.

A short time later, he opened Catherine's door and there she was propped on the pillows with her infant son in her arms. He had just been fed by the wet nurse and was content to coo and look into his mother's face. Daniel could see the dark beauty of the child and it portended a handsome man who would be dark haired and dark eyed. But at a closer look he beheld a dimple that matched one he had often noticed in his mother's cheek when she smiled, and found that indeed, he was becoming more observant.

"Good morning, or perhaps I should say good afternoon, as it seems that both of us have slept the morning away. Or some of it at least, for I know you were pretty busy until the last half. How do you feel this morning?" he inquired.

"Magnificent, and isn't my Jonathan the most beautiful child that was ever created?" She laughed.

And indeed, it might be so, Daniel noted, for, as he had thought himself, the child was beautiful.

"And here it is New Year's Eve and you will have no companion at the celebration. I am so sorry for ruining our little party this way." She sighed.

"Nonsense, don't think of it at all, I will pass my time with you tonight here and we shall see the New Year in together. Would that I could spend them all with you," he said.

"Kind sir, you would soon tire of the duty of mother and son and all the problems and chores that that would entail."

"You think me so shallow then that I could not endure those types of hardships, that I wouldn't cheerfully take them on if allowed to do so," he declared. "You abuse me to think so."

"I am sorry, of course, you are kindness personified. Forgive me for harshly judging you, but my experience with men is limited and I tend to lump all of them together. There is a favor I would ask of you again though."

"Anything, you have only to say it," he said.

"This will be a harder thing to do than any I have asked before," she stated. "I must alert the child's father of his birth and I cannot do this myself now. Will you carry a book to him for me and see if he requires a question of you how you came by it? Then you can let him know of his son and me and he can decide whether he will come and claim us," she said.

"Yes, I will, for I have long wanted to meet this man whom you have given yourself to and who is somewhere other than at your side at a time like this," he said.

"Please don't be angry or bitter, for I am sure if I had sent for him he would have come but my pride prevented me. Let us both be chastised then."

Daniel dropped beside her bed, and took her hand. "Never you, my love, you are all a man could hope for. Do not chastise yourself or distress yourself, I will take the book and give the message. Perhaps it may be to my advantage to do so, for if he comes not, I shall steal you for myself." And he raised the hand to his lips and kissed it.

"Oh, Daniel, I am so very fond of you and always have been, but don't press me now," Catherine cried.

"Where is the book, I will pack a bag and as soon as it is safe to leave you I will go."

"It is on the table by the window," she said.

"But I will only go after the doctor has been to see you."

"I understand, and it is soon enough. I think now that I must rest again. Would you have the nurse take Jonathan now and put him in his bed."

And with that the nurse came and took the child, and Daniel left her to sleep. Before she slept, she called the nurse to bring her another book from the closet and took the paper that the doctor had given her along with another scrap of paper and folded them together. Then having the nurse bring her a pen, ink, penknife, and mucilage from the drawer of the chest in the room, she slit the top of the back page between the leather cover and the glued-down page and slid the folded papers into the opening. Next she reglued the paper to the leather cover and smoothed the cover flat. Finally she penned a note inside the front fly sheet to her son. That being finished she asked the nurse to put it beneath the mattress of his cradle and, content that all was done that could be done, she drifted off to sleep.

CHAPTER SEVENTEEN

New Year's Day, 1848

New Year's, what a new year beginning, a son to comfort her in her old age and all the future ahead of her. How she would like to write today. The New Year's Eve night had gone well and though she couldn't get up and dance, she had enjoyed the quiet strength of Daniel at her side and her child sleeping in his cradle. She knew no matter what, this child would not want for a father figure. Even if Edgar refused to return, Daniel would be a mainstay in her life. She had no worries about the future now. One of them would be there and she would take what God offered her.

Today she felt well enough to get up, but the doctor had forbidden it so she would stay in bed. She would write in bed. She asked for her writing materials and bed desk to be brought. Now she could tell of her feelings for her son and for Daniel and what she envisioned the rest of her life to be. She spent the better part of the morning indulging in her creative imagination and was almost finished by the time the trays for lunch were brought. She had graduated to solid food now and was only moderately hungry. It was hard to have an appetite when you lay in bed, without the exercise to tempt you to hunger.

Daniel came into the room to check on her and saw her finishing her lunch. She had bright spots on her cheeks and her eyes were somewhat bloodshot, but he put it down to the food and thought no more about it. They spent the afternoon together and then the dinner hour before he left her to rest once more.

It wasn't until very late that night that the cry was raised and the maid rushed into his room to wake him.

"Come quick, sir, it's Miss Catherine, she is raging with the fever and I can't wake her!" the maid cried.

Daniel rushed into her room to the bed and felt her forehead. Yes, she was hot with fever and her skin was red as fire. He pulled the bedclothes from her to cool her body and the stench almost overcame him.

"Send for the doctor right away, something is very wrong," he said as he covered her again, "and bring cool cloths to bathe her body. Hurry, hurry, not a moment can be lost."

They worked frantically to cool her fever and bring her back to consciousness, but nothing worked and finally in the early morning dawn with the sound of the winter surf crashing outside, her spirit left her and she was gone.

Daniel lay upon her bed holding her lifeless body and sobbed uncontrollably, while her infant son lay nearby softly cooing.

November 14, 2001

The next morning as they were taking their coffee in the library and looking again at the poetry books of the night before, they heard the doorbell buzzing. Marissa ran to disable the alarm, while Jeff crossed the hall to answer the door. There on the porch stood Detective McGuire.

"Come in, come in, Detective, we were just having a cup of coffee, would you like one?" Jeff asked.

"No thank you, but I wanted to come and let you know what we found out last night in our questioning of your kidnapper."

"Well, come into the library and tell us all about it." The two men crossed to the library and had just seated themselves as Marissa came around the doorway. Surprised to see Stephen, she came into the room to discover what was going on.

"Honey, Detective McGuire is here with information for us about the crime. Sit down and let's listen to what he has to say," Jeff said.

"Well, after I left you at the hospital, I went back to the office and the questioning had been going on for a while. It seems that the kidnapper was afraid that he was going to take the whole wrap for the crime and wanted to work a deal with the DA's office. We got them out of bed and he finally confessed to the crime but implicated a woman, a Madeline LaCrux, an antique book collector, who had been doing some research into the life of Edgar Allan Poe. She traced his family and then started tracing the line of his sister down to the present day. It seems that down that line there was a book of poetry, which the family had claimed belonged to Edgar Allan Poe and which he had in his possession at the time of his death. His sister had come into possession of it when she made the burial arrangements for Edgar. Well, this book came down through the family and the collector had gotten hold of it from them. Noticing the number of copies published was small, she determined to get hold of as many copies as she could. She figured that they would be worth a lot of money, just like you did, and she was out to get as many as she could. When we picked her up, she confessed and told us the same story. So you folks can stop worrying about any further danger.

"Now, I am going to have to have the two books that you have for evidence and, Marissa, when the trial is over I will return your copy to you. I don't know what will happen to the other copy, probably be turned over to some museum or other. And that is the whole story of why you were kidnapped. Except for one strange thing, Marissa. Remember when you wrote the poem that you recited to the kidnapper on the phone?"

"Yes," she said.

"Well, we found a piece of paper on the floor of the kitchen of the farmhouse where Jeff was kept. And the kidnapper said that the woman had only given him one poem. He was surprised that you quoted it word for word when he hadn't even given you the title yet."

Marissa looked at Stephen and then at Jeff. They had always been on the same wavelength. She said, "Jeff, how did you know it was the poem?"

"The kidnapper read it to me before we went to call you," he said. "It must have been the kidnapper you heard when you were asleep instead of me. Or you were listening through my ears. I am going to have to be more careful when I think of things in the future if you have started reading my mind." He laughed.

"Well, thanks, Detective McGuire, for coming to tell us, here are the books, and just let us know when you need our testimony," Jeff said.

"Yes, thanks, Detective McGuire, for coming by," Marissa said with a long look.

Stephen shook both their hands, holding Marissa's a little longer than Jeff's, and then left them to their coffee.

He walked down the front walk to his car, putting the books into the seat beside him and drove away.

February 1848

Daniel sat on the deck of Captain Smith's vessel and thought back on the past days. Catherine's death, the funeral and reading of the will that she had written, the Smiths' guardianship of Jonathan and their moving into Seacliff. It was all accomplished as she had asked, and now there was but one thing left for him to do, deliver the book as she had asked and have his say to Edgar Allan Poe.

It didn't matter whether or not Poe had been there; she would still have died. It didn't matter that she was happy with her son to the end. All that mattered to him was that he had loved her beyond anything else in this world and now she was lost to him forever. He would have his say, of that you could be sure.

It was a short sail to Norfolk harbor and, upon receiving directions from Captain Smith where he might find the newspaper where Edgar worked, he set out to go there, the book inside his coat. He boarded a train to take him to Richmond. It was late that day when they pulled into the city. He relied on the cabbies to find the newspaper. They directed him and presently he came to the street. It was by now the end of February 1848, and even though he was in the south now, the chill was still in the air. He entered the door of the newspaper and made his way to the typesetter area, asking for Mr. Edgar Allan Poe as he went. He was instructed to take the stairs and at the end of the hall on the second floor he would find his office.

Daniel began to climb the stairs, the anger beginning to bubble inside him. At the end of the hall, he hammered at the door. "Come in, come in, don't break the door down," he heard the voice inside call.

There, seated at the desk, with copy spread across it, was Edgar Allan Poe. He looked terrible with bloodshot eyes, the aging of the past year showing over his face like a map. Daniel opened his coat and took out the book and threw it on the desk in front of him.

"What is this that you are throwing at me?" he demanded, picking up the book and looking at the cover. He opened it and saw that he recognized the writer's style. Then he closed the book and looked at the spine. The author's name jumped out at him, Catherine Aurora Barrett-Poe. "What is this?" he asked. "Catherine and I were never married. I would not saddle her with a wreck like me."

"That is the truth, man, but you have killed her just the same!" Daniel cried. "You miserable excuse for a man. She bore your son and now lays dead from childbed fever. She asked me to bring the book, and I have, and now I am done with you." And he turned on his heel to leave.

"But wait, what of my son then, what of him?" Edgar rushed after him.

"He awaits you at Seacliff," Daniel replied. "If you are man enough to come for him."

After Leaving Marissa and Jeffrey Delclare's Residence

When Stephen arrived at the sheriff's office, he went straight to the Property Clerk/Evidence Office and handed the officer inside the cage the books.

"Here, tag these for trial evidence in the Delclare kidnapping case. I am going back to my office to write up the report."

The office was empty of officers when Stephen finally arrived back at work. It was going to be a long day and an even longer night and he felt physically drained from the events of the past two days. He pulled open his desk drawer to get the forms he would need to write the report and a pen, looking at the two volumes of poetry that lay there among his papers. He was determined to hang on to these volumes after the trial was over. They may have Catherine Aurora Barrett-Poe's name on the cover but he knew them to be Marissa's. He would have something from her after all. He started to fill out the forms. It was going to be hard to be objective in this case. It was almost impossible to separate his feelings from the bare facts, but he must try and write an indifferent view of the whole crime. He leaned back in his chair trying to collect his thoughts and glanced at his in-basket. There in the basket was an envelope. He reached for it and slowly opened the letter. Inside there was a single piece of paper with a poem written to him. It was unsigned just as the envelope had no return address on it. Just the title and the poem:

Timeless

When dew-kissed breezes start to blow
I dream of summer's coming
My thoughts, filled with summers past
Listen to raindrops drumming.

To once again smell the scent of green,
To fill my eyes with sun, and then
To gaze on scenes of field and stream
Washed clean by spring's soft rain.

To lie in hay piled to my knees
To ride in quiet star-filled night
To take a hand in troubled need
And hold it firm and tight.

To carefully guide each faltering step
Along life's rugged, twisted road
Until I find a sheltered steppe
Where I may gently rest my load.

I've learned, though hard the lessons be,
To make merry through my cares
And tempt not Fate, harsh master, he,
To try my simples wares.

But always plodding onward, up
I change the scenes I meet
And leave them not the same
As when I set my feet.

For every step will shake the ground
And every sigh will swell the air
And when I've passed the sound
Will still be hanging breathless there.

So human experience will always leave,
Behind it lonely in its space,
A haunting memory left with reprieve
Of having once touched and held your face.

Folding the piece of paper slowly into small squares, Stephen put it into his billfold and turned out the light. The room was dim and empty with the blinds and door closed, and no one could see the smile on his lips or the tears in his eyes.

EPILOGUE

Some Days Later

"Honey, will you get the door?" Marissa shouted to Jeff as she twisted off the shower knob and proceeded to grab a towel and dry herself off. She had heard the buzzing of the doorbell even over the running water. "Jeff, are you getting it?"

"I got it, Marissa, I was in the basement," he called from downstairs in the front hall.

When he opened the door, he was surprised to see a perfect stranger staring back at him. Seeing her obvious surprise also, he said, "Can I help you, young lady?" The woman standing before him was younger than he, and quite beautiful, with arresting blue eyes and the most luxurious head of wavy black hair he had seen in a long time. She smiled back at him and asked if there was a Marissa Delclare at this address. She looked at a piece of paper on top of the bible she was holding in her hand and then again at him. He had thought that she might be a Jehovah's Witness come to evangelize until she mentioned his wife by name.

"There certainly is, that's my wife, my name is Jeffery Delclare, by the way. Won't you come in; my wife won't be a moment. I'm afraid you have caught her unawares, she is just finishing her shower."

"Oh, I am sorry, I should have called first, but when I got your names from the detective, I hurried right over. Please forgive me for interrupting. Perhaps I could come back at a better time," she stammered.

"And you are?" Jeff asked.

"Oh, forgive me, my name is Ruth Warren." At first Jeff was not quite sure where he had heard the name before, and then he remembered. The daughter of the woman who died. The real owner of the book.

Marissa finished dressing and started downstairs when she heard the voices in the hall. Ruth Warren. Catherine Barret-Poe's descendent. She wondered what the woman wanted. But she thought she knew.

187

"Hello," she said as she finished descending the stairs and held out her hand to the woman. "I wondered if we would get to meet you." Marissa smiled her welcome.

"Hello," returned Ruth. "I needed to talk with you and when I spoke with the detective at the sheriff's department, he thought you might be willing to talk with me."

"Of course, please come in and make yourself comfortable. We were just about to have coffee, may I fix some for you as well?" Marissa asked.

"I don't want to interrupt anything. I told your husband, I can come back later, if it would be better."

"Nonsense, now is just fine and we would be delighted to have you share coffee with us or perhaps a cup of tea if that would suit you better."

"A cup of tea would be wonderful, thank you so much," Ruth answered as she settled herself in a chair in the library, clutching her bible to her. She looked around the room at the bookshelves filled with books; this might not be so easy. This couple obviously loved books and might not be so easy to persuade.

Jeff sat across from her and studied the woman's face while Marissa left to prepare the cups. He watched as she looked from shelf to shelf, as if searching for something.

"It isn't there, you know," he said.

"What isn't there?" she said.

"The book you're looking for. It isn't there."

"I was just noticing how many books you have here. It must be wonderful to own so many," she answered pensively.

"Do you like books, also?" He tried again to draw her out.

"Oh, yes, I have always loved books. I remember the first book I ever had. It was Jack London's *White Fang*. I only had that one for many years, and I read it over and over again.

"A great book, I agree, I think I still have my copy here somewhere," Jeff answered and then stood up to help his wife bring in the coffee and tea things and set them on a table nearby.

"And so, Ruth, you are here about the book," Marissa answered, direct as always, "I suppose."

"I know I don't have any right to ask, but I was wondering if you would sell it back to me. I don't have a lot of money but I could pay you so much for a number of years if that would be all right. I feel so bad letting it get away from me in the first place. Mother meant for me to have it since I was very young and I never felt I should say anything to anyone until she was gone. I never dreamed that my stepsisters would have the house sold and everything liquidated in such a short time.

"When I returned from my trip to find everything sold and the house occupied by strangers, I was heartbroken. I questioned them about the book, but they couldn't remember who had bought it. They did mention a couple of bidders but that was all. It was just a book to them. They wouldn't have known the significance of it. Just a miscellaneous title on a jot ticket and a price."

Marissa listened to the tale and felt more sorry for the young woman than she could bear. A tie to her history gone to strangers. Something to pass down to her children someday, something that her mother had entrusted her to care for when she was gone. She looked at Jeff and she saw the understanding in his eyes. Yes, it was a treasure and they were the legal owners of it, but it really belonged to this young woman.

"I am sorry, I can't give the book to you right now," Marissa began.

"Oh please, name your price, I will get it somehow, I know the book is very valuable in a collector's world, but I will find a way to reimburse you."

"It isn't the money, Ruth, we don't want the money from you. The book clearly belongs to you and if I had it I would give it to you. But the sheriff's department has it locked up for evidence in the trial. When it is returned to me, I will see that you have it back," Marissa said.

"Oh, thank you so much, you don't know what this means to me," Ruth rejoiced. "I do have my mother's bible and our family is recorded there if you are interested."

The excitement leaped into Marissa's eyes. To see the connections would be wonderful.

"Yes, I really would like to see it," she exclaimed drawing closer to the chair the young woman was seated on.

"See, here is Catherine's birthdate and her mother's name and birth and death dates. Then here is Jonathan's name and the marriages and births and deaths right on down to my grandparents and my mother's and her child. I am adopted by her second husband," Ruth explained. "So you can imagine what a treasure it is to me and the book brings it all together."

"I think I do, but I would ask a favor of you, let my company have the rights to publish the book as a reprint so that the rest of the world can enjoy it as well. You, of course, will be given royalties as the descendent of the author," Jeff answered.

"Yes, I can see how valuable this would be. Can you chart it for us so that when your new edition comes out we can include it?" Marissa questioned.

"You mean, you can do that for me?"

"In fact, we will be overjoyed to do it for you, and also allow us to include the birth certificate and letter from your author-ancestor in the book reprint."

"I didn't know about the birth certificate or letter until the detective spoke of them. Of course, that would be wonderful. Thank you so much, Mr. Delclare."

"Just call me, Jeff," he said, "since we are going into business together."

Ruth stood up beside herself with happiness. Her book would be published and her great, great, great, great grandmother would be made famous. She smiled her widest and shook both their hands and then making her good-byes left them smiling at each other.

Jeff looked at Marissa. "Well, all's well that ends well."

"I knew you would understand why I had to give it back to her. If it hadn't been for her and her information to the sheriff's office we might never have found out for sure about the connection to the book, and without the connection the kidnapping made no sense. I feel that she played a key role in my getting you back and that's all I was worried about," Marissa said.

"It was the right thing to do, darling, and the right thing to do is always best." He smiled.